Sheila's Dying

Sheila's Dying

ALDEN R. CARTER

G. P. Putnam's Sons

New York

ACKNOWLEDGMENTS

Many thanks to all who helped with *Sheila's Dying*, especially my agent, Ray Puechner, my sister, Cynthia Carter LeBlanc, and my friends Dean Markwardt, Jack Bittrich, Gary Diamond, Judy and Alain Roy, Sue Babcock, and Georgette Frazer. I am particularly indebted to my mother, Hilda Carter Fletcher, my advisers Don Beyer and Dr. Michel Roy, and, of course, my wife, Carol.

Book design by Alice Lee Groton
Printed in the United States of America
First impression
Library of Congress Cataloging-in-Publication Data
Carter, Alden R. Sheila's dying.
Summary: Just as high school junior Jerry Kinkaid is considering breaking up with his girlfriend, he discovers that she has a terminal case of cancer. [1. Cancer—Fiction. 2. Death—Fiction.] I. Title.
PZ7.C2426Sh 1987 [Fic] 86-25129
ISBN 0-399-21405-4

ONE

Late in the winter of Sheila's dying, I tried to remember why I'd hated the Tiger.

Bonnie Harper was at it again: "Where is it carved in stone that it's an athletic letter? It's a school letter, and kids who work their butts off in band, drama, forensics, and other activities deserve it too. It would make them proud to go to this school. It would bring everyone closer together."

She'd tried the school unity number on us before, and not a face on my side of the table changed expression. The four other kids in Bonnie's delegation looked just as bored. She gave me what I suppose was her "let-us-reason-together" look. I sighed. "You try it this time, Phil. I'm too tired."

Phil Colburn, who'd been staring morosely at the clock, said, "Huh. Oh, ya. Right. Look, Bonnie, it's an athletic letter. It's always been an athletic letter. What's the point of changing?" He went on with our standard argument, and I

7

stopped listening. It was a beautiful day for the middle of November in Wisconsin, and I wanted out of the school. I'd drive south of town and take a walk along the river. Then supper and the game. Marston wasn't supposed to be much good, so I might even get some decent playing time. That'd be a change.

"Mr. Chairman, I'd like to call a motion." Bonnie was staring at me with ill-concealed dislike.

"O.k. Go ahead." She did, then wound a thin coil of hair around a forefinger and chewed on the end as we voted. I counted the ballots. Stalemate: five for, five against. Big surprise.

Bonnie sighed and was about to go at it again, but Phil was too quick for her. "I move that we adjourn."

"Hey, the final bell hasn't even rung," Bonnie yelped. "We've got the room until four. Come on, let's get this worked out."

"It's Friday, for cripes sake," Phil said. "Some of us have things to do."

He emphasized the *some* and Bonnie reddened. For a second I felt a little sorry for her. She wasn't bad-looking— a good figure, dark clear skin, and the hint of Indian blood in her features. Still, what guy wanted a girl with an IQ of about 200 and the personality of a tiger shark? "Do I hear a second?" I asked.

"I've got to go to the bathroom. I'll second it," Jill Sikes said from Bonnie's side of the table. Bonnie glared at her.

"Well, maybe we can pass something today," I said. "Do we need a secret ballot this time, Bonnie?"

"Yes, that's what we agreed at the start of the hour." Her voice was tight with anger. Everybody else groaned and started to object.

"Come on, cool it. Let's just get it over with," I said and called the vote. Nine to one. You couldn't say that Bonnie gave up easily.

8

Phil and I walked down the ramp from the administration wing. "There goes another wasted hour," Phil said. "I could have gotten half my homework done. At this rate, we'll be meeting all winter. What are we going to do?"

"Beats me." I wasn't interested in talking about it. All I wanted to do was get by myself for a while. I was scoping out the weather through the windows. A wind was up in the west, driving puffy clouds across a sky of autumn blue. Down by the river, the air would be sharp with frost and the smell of fallen leaves.

"We've got to get some of her people aside and try to convince them. All we need is one vote," Phil said.

"You'd better have the bucks for a big bribe."

"Ya, to leave to their next of kin. Bonnie's going to kill anyone who votes with us."

I shook my head. "No, they're not afraid of Bonnie. Those guys really believe. They elected Bonnie because they figured she could bulldoze us."

"Well, she can't, and we're not having any luck convincing them. So what do we do next?"

"Maybe I'll just tell the principal that we can't agree."

"Ya, and then they'll stop listening to what kids say about anything."

"Phil, just drop it, huh? We'll try to work out something next week, but now I'm just sick of talking about it."

Phil shrugged. "Well, maybe Bonnie will get run over by a truck or something this weekend. . . . After the game, some of the guys are going over to Junction to check out the band at the Purple Horse. Want to come?"

"I'm meeting Sheila. Maybe we'll drive over."

He grinned at me. "You know, for a guy who always said he was gonna play it loose, you've gotten whipped pretty good."

"Phil, goddamn it—"

He laughed. "Take it easy. Just kidding you. I know it's

9

just casual, but when are you going to tell Sheila that?"

"I don't need to tell her. Now just can it, Phil. I'm not in the mood."

The final bell rang while we were getting our books from our lockers. Damn Bonnie for that last secret ballot; now we'd have to fight the crowd. "Hey, Jerr-o!" Sheila's voice.

Phil smirked. "I'll see you at the game."

She came prancing up. I said, "I thought you had a dentist's appointment."

She sucked in her cheeks. "Yep. They pulled all my teeth and sent me back to school." I had to smile; Sheila was a great clown. She caught me by the arm and grinned wide, showing her even, white teeth. "Look, no cavities. Sheila Porter's record of sixteen years of flawless checkups still stands."

"That would make you nineteen or twenty. They don't start giving checkups until you're three or so."

"Details. Record still stands. Where we goin'?" I shrugged. We started walking toward the parking lot. "Hey, is my guy in one of his moods? Need some cheering up, Jerr-o?" She gave my arm a squeeze. "Let's drive down to that spot by the river."

What the hell, I'd been going there anyway. And Sheila was beginning to do what she usually did to me.

Two miles below the dam, the river stretched broad and smooth. On the south side of the highway bridge, I turned down a gravel road running parallel to the river. I knew Sheila was humoring me. She no more wanted to walk through the woods to sit by the river than I wanted to chair another meeting on the letters issue.

We sat in the shelter of a granite outcropping and watched the river flow. On the opposite shore, the hospital sat on a low bluff, its windows reflecting the clouds and sky.

Sheila snuggled in against me, and I put an arm around her. "How was Bonnie today?" she asked.

"Your friend was, as usual, a major pain in the ass."

"Oh, she's not so bad."

"So you keep telling me. What the hell do you see in her anyway? You're not anything alike."

Sheila shrugged. "Oh, I don't know. Maybe I've just got strange taste in people." She grinned. "After all, I'm hooked on you, Jerr-o. Maybe you two are more alike than you think."

I grimaced. "Careful. I may be tempted to violence."

She laughed at me, but for once she didn't seem interested in a blow-by-blow account of my latest run-in with Bonnie. We didn't talk for a couple of minutes. I relaxed, listening to the wind high in the trees. Sheila seemed intent on separating the seeds from a dry pine cone. "Jerr-o, I think we ought to go steady."

This again. "Come on, Sheila. You know I don't go for that ring stuff. We're doing o.k. I'm not planning on going out with anyone else."

She snuggled in a little closer. "It would just make me feel better if, you know, I didn't have to worry about someone like Bonnie grabbing you."

"Bonnie?" I yelled. Sheila rolled on top of me, going for the ticklish spot below my ribs. She was strong and limber, and it took me a couple of minutes before I had her pinned. She was giggling and out of breath. "Bonnie Harper," I said, "is the last girl in the Western Hemisphere I'd ask out."

"Kiss me, you fool." I did, releasing her arms. Suddenly she was hanging on to me and sobbing. "Oh, Jerr-o, Jerr-o. Promise me you won't leave me for her. I couldn't live without you. Oh, please don't leave me, Jerr-o."

I groaned. "Come on, Sheila, give me a break."

She pulled back and grinned. "Not bad, huh? Think I'll be a star?"

"I think they're going to put you in the nuthouse one of these days."

She jerked upright. "What a thing to say!" She addressed an unseen audience. "This guy here. This boyfriend of mine—steady boyfriend, I'll have you know—tells me I'm crazy. Now how's that supposed to make a girl feel?"

I leaned back against the granite and closed my eyes. "It makes the boyfriend feel tired."

She dropped the act and hugged me. "You love it, and you know it." I grunted, not opening my eyes. "How about it, Jerr-o? Can I at least tell my girlfriends that I'm going steady with Jerry Kinkaid, star guard of the Conklin basketball team?"

"Star bench-warmer maybe."

"That'll do." She swung around and yelled, "Hey, everybody, Sheila Porter is now officially the steady girlfriend of Jerry Kinkaid, star bench-warmer of the—"

I had her, one hand over her mouth. "You are demented, Sheila! Are you high on drugs or something?" She bit a finger. "Ouch."

"I'm just high on you, Steady."

I leaned back again. "I have had one hell of a long day, and now I've got a crazy woman on my hands. O.k., o.k, you can tell your friends that we're going steady. Almost steady. Just let me relax for a couple of minutes, or I won't have energy for the game." She caressed my forehead and started humming a lullaby which I knew was headed for a much higher volume. "Sheila, I'm warning you . . ."

She giggled and relaxed into my arms. For a few minutes she was quiet. I listened to the wind and the river. A nuthatch landed on a pine and stared at us, then disappeared in a whir. Cars crossed the bridge upstream, the rush of their passing echoing faintly to us. I felt my pulse slowing. I was cooling out, getting things back in perspective—Bonnie, the letters thing, the trig test on Monday. None of those things counted for much. I'd get everything worked out. The game wouldn't count for much either. If I played, I'd turn on the adrenaline and work my butt off. If I didn't play, well, what the hell.

Sheila had accused me of being "drugged-out" on nature. That was taking it a little far. I could get into parties, music, and loud good times, but sometimes I needed to get away from things—let the rattling around in my head settle a bit. Not Sheila. She wanted to keep the accelerator down hard all the time. She'd party every night if she had the chance.

A lot of our friends probably thought it pretty odd that we were going together. I know Phil did. I was a country boy, Sheila a townee. I kept a high B average while Sheila didn't give a damn about schoolwork and dragged in with a low C. I got asked to sit on committees and had been vice-president of the sophomore class. Sheila hung with a crowd that couldn't have cared less about grades or student government—scoring the next beer, cigarette, or joint concerned them a lot more.

Then why were we going together? Later I spent a lot of time trying to figure that out. To begin with, she was damn good-looking: tall, blond, and built. So far she hadn't let me investigate the finer points of her architecture, but there were consolations. She made me laugh, got me out of my occasional funks. I appreciated that, felt loose and easy in her company.

And Sheila? Hell, I don't know. God knows there were enough other guys ready to ask her out. Maybe she thought of me as a challenge, a tough audience for her performances. Still, I think there was something more too. Maybe she needed me to lean on, to calm her down some. I'm not sure. All I know is that we were relaxed and comfortable in each other's arms that afternoon on the riverbank across from the hospital.

At that time we'd been going out for a couple of months. We'd gotten started pretty much by chance. I'd never paid much attention to her until the fall of my junior year. I'd seen her around, knew her name, and liked how she looked, but Conklin High has some 650 kids, and we'd never been in each other's crowds.

Early in September, I went with Phil and some of the other guys to the first football game of the season. (I'd never gone out for the team because the season spanned some of the best hunting and fishing weeks of the year.) The reigning conference champions were in town, and we all expected Conklin to get shellacked good. Instead, we played them tough all game and trailed by three with a minute to go. Jim Frieborg, our quarterback, completed two to get us to their thirty, then got sacked on the forty. No time for a huddle. Frieborg dropped back and heaved the ball as far as he could. Mike Bowker slipped out of nowhere, made a leaping catch, juked two defenders, and cruised into the end zone.

The crowd went absolutely nuts. In the row in front of me, Sheila and half a dozen other girls were yelling and screaming at the top of their lungs. It seemed natural enough that we should all go out and celebrate. We piled into our cars. By chance, Sheila got squeezed in beside me. She got us howling with this insane replay of the last few plays of the game. God, she was funny. We stopped at the bowling alley for pizza. Sheila kept us laughing with outrageous plans for the rest of the evening: "We should paint the water tower purple with big green and pink stripes. I mean, can you imagine what would happen? People driving up the highway would just blow lunch! They'd turn around or find a detour. This town would be empty in two days. We'd take over!"

Phil reached over for Sheila's glass and took a swallow. "Yep. Straight bourbon. Cheap stuff too. No wonder the girl's unhinged. I think we ought to bowl a few lines."

"But guys," Sheila protested, "we're missing the perfect chance. We're on a roll, let's push it. After we get done with the water tower, we can paint the steam engine in the park purple."

"Where are we going to get all this purple paint?" I asked.

"Details. You be in charge of that. Everyone says you're a good detail guy: a bit slow to get the big picture, but great with the details." I raised my eyebrows, mildly offended. She winked at me.

The pizza was gone, and Phil was arranging for the alleys. He could only get two, so some of us had to sit out every other game. I bowled a pretty good game, although I was rusty. Sheila was terrible at first. I could tell she hadn't bowled much, but she took the game seriously and started concentrating. She was tall and strong, and her coordination was good. By the fourth or fifth frame she was hitting the pocket well. I was impressed—and attracted.

At the end of the game, I said to her, "Nice job. You really got your score up."

She gave me an odd look, almost like she didn't remember we'd been sitting together half the evening. "Thanks." She headed for the restaurant half of the building.

After maybe ten minutes, I wandered out to see what had happened to her. She wasn't in the restaurant, so I went out to the parking lot. She was leaning against the hood of my car with her arms crossed over her stomach. "You feeling all right?" I asked. She looked pale.

"Oh, I'm o.k. I felt a little sick to my stomach for a couple of minutes. It happens sometimes when I've been laughing a lot."

"Do you want a 7-Up or something?"

"No, just fresh air. Let's take a walk." We strolled down the main street, talking about school, classes, and so on. She started to feel better and began doing imitations of a few of the teachers. She was good at it, and I laughed until it was my stomach that hurt.

The siren at the fire station howled. In a couple of minutes, the trucks came roaring up the street. They turned off and pulled to a stop next to the farm-implement dealership a block from the river. "Let's go watch!" Sheila grabbed my hand and pulled me toward the scene.

Conklin only has around 8,000 people, and there are just enough full-time firemen to drive the trucks. Volunteers with pagers make up the rest of the department. Soon cars and pickups were screeching in from other parts of town. Several guys got the door open and charged inside with hoses, axes, and all sorts of good stuff. But there was no fire. The owner showed up about then, and the fire chief laid into him about the alarm system going haywire three times in a month. Most of the firemen stood around glaring at the scene as if they were about to lynch the owner or burn the place down just so a faulty alarm wouldn't screw up another Friday evening. Sheila loved it. She stood holding on to my arm and watching everything. I could tell she was putting together a fantastic version to tell later.

Finally things settled down, and we started walking back toward the bowling alley. At the corner of Birch and Third, she said, "I live down here a couple of blocks. I think I'll walk home."

"Don't you want to go back to the bowling alley?"

"Nope, not tonight. Got a little headache. But thanks for the walk, Jerr-o."

16

"What did you call me?"

"Jerr-o. I do that to people I like. I change their names a little bit. It makes those people more mine."

"Oh, o.k., I guess. I like you too." I fumbled a bit. "So, anyway, got plans for tomorrow night?"

"Just going out with you."

"Well, great. What shall we do?"

"Suggest something outrageous."

It was a test. "Ah . . . go skinny-dipping."

She dug me in the ribs. "I knew you had it in you. Good idea, but not on the first date."

"Well, we can count this as the first. Besides, it might be too cold in a week or two."

"I'll think about it. When do you want to pick me up?"

Of course, we didn't go skinny-dipping the next night. We did have a great time, though, and after that we went out two or three times a week. It was months before I saw her feel sick again.

TWO

I dropped Sheila off and got home in time for a quick bite. I hated not being able to have a good meal before a game—I was five ten, 160 pounds, and growing—but I played by the rules and had only orange juice and toast.

My sister, Melissa, spent most of supper bitching about her algebra teacher, saying that I was lucky I'd had Page as a freshman. I didn't argue. Melissa would bring home an A as usual, although it beat me how she could be so smart with a feather duster for a brain.

Mom looked tired. She'd been pulling the graveyard shift at the mill for several weeks, and it was tough on her. "Are you working this weekend, Mom?"

"I'm not sure. They said there might be some overtime available tomorrow night."

"If it's not mandatory, maybe you ought to let somebody else take it. You look bushed."

"Oh, I'm o.k., but I think I'd better get a couple of hours' sleep instead of listening to the game."

"Sure, Mom. It won't be much of a game."

"Attitude, that's your problem," Melissa said. "You shouldn't say that. You ought to be getting psyched up. This could be your big night to show them what you can do. You don't want to sit on the bench all next year too."

"I may not even be on the team next year, Mel. There are a lot of good guys on the JV squad. Besides, I may have more important things to do as a senior." Melissa gave a sigh of disgust. I ignored her.

"We got a letter from your father today," Mom said.

"What did he want?" I asked.

"Nothing. He just wrote to say he'd been transferred to Seattle. He suggested that you two fly out for a visit in June."

"Well, I wouldn't mind seeing Seattle, but I'm not much interested in seeing him."

Melissa butted in. "That's what I said. I mean, where does he get off, anyway? If he wants to do something for us, why doesn't he send the support checks on time? I think we ought to hire a lawyer."

Mom sighed. "He's got his own family to support too, Melissa. Don't be too hard on him. Someday I think it would be nice if you children got to know him a little."

Neither one of us remembered Dad or cared either. He'd left Mom when I was two and a half and Melissa was about six months. He was a foreman at the mill, and when there was a layoff that fall, he'd said he was going out West to look for a better job. He never came back. Eventually, Mom got the divorce papers in the mail. He didn't dispute custody and let Mom have almost all the money and property. I'll hand it to him for that. He remarried soon after and had three or four kids. Every Christmas he sent Melissa and me five bucks apiece. We sent him a card. Profit: ten dollars minus the cost of the card and a postage stamp.

It sounds like I was bitter. I wasn't really. We lived in the house Mom's father left her, and she made a pretty good buck at the mill. I worked in the summer, so I could buy my own clothes and keep my Dodge chugging along. I was willing to work part-time during the winter too, but Mom said no: "You take care of the grades. I'll worry about the money. Once you're through the first couple of years in college, you can worry about both. And when I'm too old to work, you two can support me."

With Mom working such long hours, Melissa and I had grown up pretty independent. We'd long since worked out a routine so Mom didn't have to worry about most of the cooking, cleaning, and washing. (Hell, I knew more about that stuff than most girls did.) And we didn't take problems to her we could solve ourselves. We made out o.k. and were proud of it.

I knew kids who had it a lot rougher—Sheila, for instance. Her parents had died in a charter airplane crash when she was an infant. Everyone on board was killed except Sheila, who was found without a scratch. No wonder she had kind of a weird view of life sometimes. She grew up in her grandparents' home and took their name. Old man Porter was a pharmacist, so he had a decent income for this part of the world. He died when Sheila was twelve, leaving them something to live on, but not a lot. Mrs. Porter sold the house, and they moved into a smaller place. The old lady started slipping after that. Without any relatives to help, Sheila had quite a job taking care of the house and her grandmother. So, everything considered, I hardly had reason to complain about my luck.

Melissa and I left the house a little after six and drove the five miles into town. "Jean Lewis called before you got home and asked Mom to double-date tomorrow night," she said.

"Oh, ya? I suppose Mom said no."

21

"Ya, she told me that the guy is a cigar-smoking fatty from quality control. Mom said she'd rather work than listen to him tell dirty jokes and belch."

"Too bad she doesn't get asked out by someone with a little class. She needs more social life."

"Sure, but suppose she found someone who wanted to get married. Can you imagine what kind of an idiot would take on the two of us? We don't need somebody that stupid around."

I laughed. "Well, it wouldn't be so bad if he was rich."

"Maybe if he was rich *and* old. Like real old." Melissa started describing how we might prod the mythical oldster into a premature heart attack. He was a familiar figure in our family mythology. Many times around the supper table, Melissa and I had speculated on his existence. Mom's response was consistent: "You children are not selling off your mother, no matter how good the money is." "But, Mom," we'd protest, "we'll take care of him. You won't have to worry about a thing. Just cry at the funeral." Yet, all the kidding aside, it was too bad that Mom never gave herself much of a chance with men after Dad left.

In town, we stopped to pick up one of Melissa's friends. Melissa took her bag inside, since she was coming back after the game to stay overnight. I told her to hurry; the varsity was required to watch the JV game, and I'd be late if we didn't move it.

I got to my place on the lowest row of the bleachers just at tip-off. Coach Burke wasn't there himself yet. That figured. Phil was beside me. "Freeze your ass off down by the river?" he asked.

"No, it was a nice afternoon."

"You've got strange ideas about comfort. I went home and crawled in a hot bath."

"How's the back?"

"Not bad. I'll be o.k. as long as that idiot Burke doesn't pull me and keep me out until it stiffens up."

"Careful. Here's the man himself." Coach Burke, wearing his take-no-prisoners look, stalked to the end of the row and sat. We turned our attention to the game.

Whoever had said Marston wasn't very good had definitely been full of crap. Our JVs were usually pretty respectable, but Marston's squad thumped them from the start. Marston was ahead by 23 in the middle of the fourth quarter when Burke stood and led us into the locker room. "Cripes," Phil muttered, "we'd have trouble with their JVs. Their varsity is going to eat us alive."

"Colburn, you got something to say?"

"Nothin' much, Coach. Just saying that our JVs might have had trouble, but we'll eat their varsity alive."

"Right. O.k., listen up, men." He said the usual stuff about taking it to them on the boards, keeping our hands up on defense, and how we could win this one for ol' Conklin High if we really wanted to. I doubt if anyone believed him—we'd lost the first three games of the season against teams about as good as Marston's JVs—but we had enough pride to try to get in the spirit.

Phil was something in the first half. By halftime he had 14 points, and we were actually ahead by 3. The door slammed in the third quarter. Their coach must have said something magic in the locker room, because they came out smoking. We were down by 10 at the end of the quarter, and Mike Bowker, our other starting guard, had fouled out. I got my chance then and broke my butt. Like Phil, I had a good hand that night, making three of four from the field and a couple of free throws. But they chewed us up inside, building the lead to 20 before starting to substitute. We lost by 15 and Burke had a good old time telling us how we'd let the chance for a big victory slip away. Screw you, I thought, we gave what we had. We hit the showers.

Sheila was waiting for me at the locker room door. "Great game, Jerr-o."

"In case you didn't notice, we lost."

"Ya, but I was proud to see my steady tossing the old pumpkin around like Joe DiMaggio."

"DiMaggio played baseball."

"Details. What shall we do? Want to go skinny-dipping?"

"Wise ass. You're a month and a half too late. Let's get something to eat, then drive over to the Purple Horse and check out the band."

We ate at the root beer stand advertised as the only year-round drive-in in the state. If you've been to northern Wisconsin in the winter, you'll understand why that was quite a claim. The carhops wore snowmobile suits from mid-December until March and, believe me, nobody left the tray on the window on a twenty-below night in January.

Sheila didn't seem very interested in her food, which was unusual since she usually ate as much as I did. "Do you really feel like driving over to Junction?" she asked.

"Sure, why not? It's only fifteen miles. Don't you feel up to it?"

She shrugged. "I don't know. I guess so. Ya, why not?"

At the door of the Purple Horse, I paid the cover and accepted the flyer outlining "acceptable conduct." Quick summary: no drugs, no booze. As usual, no one was paying much attention to the rules. I did—training, you know— but Sheila got her Coke spiked by a friend with a bottle of rum.

I wasn't the world's greatest dancer, but usually Sheila had me on the floor most of the evening. That night, she let up after a couple of numbers and seemed content to sit at a table in a corner of the dim, smoky room. I saw Bonnie come in the door. "Tiger, Tiger," I said.

"Huh?" Sheila said, looking toward the door.

"That's what I decided to call her this afternoon. Tiger, as in tiger shark."

"Who?"

"Bonnie."

"Oh, I see her. Hey, Bonnie! Over here."

"Cripes, Sheila, don't." I leaned back and groaned. Sometimes Sheila needed a muzzle.

Bonnie made her way through the crowd. "Hi, guys." She sat. "How's the band?"

They talked while I looked around as if I was trying to spot someone. Gary Johnson, our center and best player, dropped into a chair beside me. "Nice game, Jerry. We should have had you in there earlier. With six guys on the court, we might have beat them."

"Ya, they were rough, weren't they?"

"You got that right. I feel like I've been through a car crusher. They were really doing a number on me. I'm a forward, damn it, not a center. Why don't they bring up that big kid from the JVs?"

"I figure they want to keep that team together for next year. After you, Mike, and the other seniors graduate, the rest of us will probably get shit-canned."

"You and Colburn wouldn't make a bad backcourt. You're not as quick as Mike, but you're a better shot." He leaned down to massage his calves. "Damn, my legs are cramping up. Mind if I ask Sheila to dance? I've got to move some."

"Go ahead."

They went off to dance, and I was stuck with Bonnie. "Go to the game, Bonnie?"

"No, I volunteer at the hospital on Fridays. Did you guys earn your letters?"

I winced. That was Bonnie for you: master diplomat. "As a matter of fact, I think we did. We lost, but we busted our butts."

25

She rested her chin on a fist. "How about the kids in the pep band? Did they have a good game?"

"I don't know, Bonnie. I didn't have much time to pay attention. But I doubt if they've got the bruises and sore legs Phil and Gary have right now."

"And I see you've still got a sore head."

I leaned forward, staring hard into her dark eyes. She didn't give a millimeter. "What is it with you, Bonnie? Don't you ever let up? I'm doing the best job I can on that committee. Just because we don't agree, you don't have to make it personal."

"I think you're a stooge for the administration. They don't want the policy changed, so they appoint get-along Jerry Kinkaid as the chairman. I can hear Weathers now: 'Yep, he'll stall until all those fag artsy-craftsy yo-yos give up.'"

I looked at her in complete disbelief. "You've got to be kidding. Do you really believe I'm some kind of agent?"

"Probably not intentionally, but it amounts to the same thing. You've blocked every attempt we've made at compromise."

"Compromise! What compromise? You've been stubborn as a mule all the way through this thing."

"Classy simile, Kinkaid. Stubborn as a mule. I'm going to write that one down."

I felt my face flush. "Look, Harper, I don't need your sarcasm. Where the hell did you learn your manners, anyway? In the shark tank at some aquarium? I told Sheila we ought to call you the tiger shark."

She brushed back a lock of dark hair and gazed at a spot above my head. "Tiger shark. Hmmmm . . . I like the tiger part of it." She looked at me and smiled. "All right, you have my permission."

Permission! I don't think anyone can accuse me of having

26

a quick temper, but I almost reached across the table to grab her by the throat.

"Hi. Are you guys having a good time?" Sheila was back.

"I am," Bonnie said.

Gary plopped back in his chair. "Nice dancing with a tall girl. For once I didn't have to bend over double."

We sat there for a while. Sheila had another drink, and I was surprised when Bonnie helped herself to some of the rum when it passed between the tables. She stuck a dollar bill in among the half dozen others under the rubber band around the bottle. The owner was making a nice profit. "You're obviously not in training, Bonnie," I said.

"Nope. And I notice that you jocks aren't worried about inhaling any of the cigarette smoke floating around here."

"My God, my growth is going to be stunted!" Gary looked around in terror.

The band started to play a song Sheila liked, and she grabbed my hand. "Come on, let's dance."

I doubt if Gary wanted to dance with Bonnie, but he'd always been polite and easygoing, so he asked her. He was, I calculated, about sixteen inches taller, and they looked awkward dancing the long, slow number. I said to Sheila, "Let's take off after this song."

"Why? We've been here less than an hour."

"I'm just not in the mood to fight with Bonnie for the rest of the night."

She gave me a squeeze. "She's just got the hots for you, Steady. It's her way of showing it."

"Give me a break, will you?"

She pulled back and stared into my eyes. "You know, I'm half serious. I've caught her watching you. I think maybe she does have a crush on you."

"Horsecrap. She's fantasizing about roasting me alive. Oops."

Gary had maneuvered to run into us. "Jerry, cut in," he yelped, winked at me, and took Sheila in his arms.

Bonnie and I stared at each other, and, believe me, there was no love in her eyes. We danced well apart, gazing coolly at each other. I didn't want to get into the letters thing again, so I asked, "What kind of work do you do at the hospital?"

"I'm a Volunteen. The hospital is understaffed, so there's always lots to do. We take around magazines, talk with the patients, help the nurses, run errands, that sort of stuff."

"How long have you been doing it?"

"Two years. I enjoy it."

"Going to be a nurse?"

"That or something in community health care." She seemed about to say more, but then her eyes narrowed with suspicion. I could almost see her defenses coming up. "How about you? I gather that basketball is only a passing fancy."

I let the shot pass. "Something that keeps me outdoors. Forestry or game management, I think."

"My dad's the game warden here. Did you know that?"

"Sure. I've run into him a few times. He's a good guy." I felt like adding, "How he's got a bitch like you for a daughter, I'll never know," but I didn't.

The song ended with a rattle of drums, and we returned to the table. Gary didn't sit. "I'm going to cruise. Keep the legs moving. Thanks, Sheila."

"That sounds like a good idea," I said. "Let's go, Sheila. It's hot in here."

"O.k. See you later, Bonnie."

"Ya, bye, Bonnie."

Bonnie bared her teeth, her eyes challenging. "That's Tiger, Kinkaid. As in tiger shark."

"You got it. We'll see you, Tiger."

In the car Sheila was laughing. "You two are funny. I'd

like to see you put on helmets and go after each other with those foam-rubber clubs. Biff! Bop! Smack! Take that, Tiger! Here's one for you, Kinkaid! God, it would be great. The whole school would buy tickets."

I glared at her. "Just can it, Sheila. If you invite her to our table next time, I'll get up and leave."

Sheila leaned over and gave me a hug. "I'm sorry. I won't. Come on, give me a kiss."

"I don't feel like it."

"Well, I do!" She jumped on me and tried to wrestle her way to a kiss, at the same time digging for the ticklish spot below my ribs. Then, in spite of myself, I was laughing. I gave her the kiss, which turned into a long one. She broke it off and pecked me on the nose. "Am I forgiven?"

"Oh, I guess."

"Come on, make it sincere." She dug for my ticklish spot again.

"O.k., o.k. You're forgiven. Stop it!"

She sat back and grinned. "O.k., but just remember I'm keeping an eye on you and Bonnie. No sneaking out on me, Steady."

I let it pass. She'd keep teasing me about Bonnie as long as I showed it bothered me. I got the car started, and we turned onto the highway leading back to Conklin. The moon was high in a chill sky. "There's a ring around the moon," I said.

"What's that supposed to mean?"

"Changing weather. Snow soon."

"I hope not. I hate to see winter come."

"We could use a little snow for hunting season. You can track a hit deer a lot better with some snow on the ground."

"Are you going this year?"

"Sure. Good sport, cheap meat. Want to get a license and come along? We can find an extra rifle."

She shuddered. "No, thank you! Makes me sick to think

29

about shooting deer." I was about to give her the usual and very good arguments for deer hunting, but she saw it coming and changed the subject. "What do you want to do now?"

Good subject. "Well, Melissa's at a friend's, and Mom will be at work by now. We'd have the house to ourselves."

"Is my guy horny again?" She blew in my ear, making me jerk the steering wheel so the car swerved.

I steadied it. She nibbled my earlobe. "Why don't you save that until we get there?"

"Uh, uh. When this girl gets hot, she wants it now." She put an arm around me and started massaging my ribs.

I had to slow the car. "Damn it, Sheila. This is dangerous. Save it." I had to reach up with my right hand for a handful of hair to pull her away. She sat back, giggling. Well, tonight maybe she means it, I thought.

But she didn't. When we got to the house, she spent ten minutes finding an album she wanted to hear. After two minutes together on the couch, she wanted to dance. After that, it was time to make some popcorn. When the popcorn was gone, I thought we might be able to get serious, but then she had to see what was on the late-night movie.

When I started getting grumpy, she let herself relax for a few minutes, and I thought we might still get somewhere. But she drew the line at the third blouse button. "It's too cold in here, Jerr-o."

"I'll get a blanket."

"I'm allergic to wool."

"I'll make it cotton."

She pulled back. "Take a hint, Jerr-o. Sheila ain't ready for that yet."

I leaned back. Damn. "Ya, and when will she be ready?"

"Sometime." She gave me a squeeze and forced a kiss from me. Then she was panting in my ear. "I'm just afraid

I'd kill you. The fires in me, Jerr-o. Oh, the sweet, savage, all-consuming fires." She went for the spot below my ribs. We tumbled to the floor, and I had to pin her to keep from being tickled into hysterics.

How could you stay angry with her? She looked up at me with her eyes dancing. "Cripes," I said, "you are some piece of work."

"I know it. Look at the bright side. You're getting lots of practice in the arts of seduction."

"I'm getting lots of practice in self-defense."

"That too. You'll have a black belt in yoga before you know it."

"Yoga isn't a martial art. You mean karate or judo or something."

"Details. Let me up, Steady. Granny is expecting me home before dawn."

THREE

Tryouts for the fall play started the following week. Sheila was going to get one of the leads if it killed her. "No more bit parts, Jerr-o. This girl has a reputation to make. I'm going to be a star."

And she meant it too. All Sheila's craziness had a seriousness behind it. She really was intent on being an actress. But a lot of her usual ease left her when she stepped onstage. Her movements got awkward, and she'd flub lines she'd spent hours memorizing. After the second night, she called me in tears. "Jerr-o, I was awful! I stumbled. I mean, I actually stumbled just walking across the stage. And then I couldn't remember anything. I'll never get a part. If I'm lucky, they'll let me sweep up after the play."

"I'm sure it wasn't that bad."

"It was worse! Just ask anyone. Ask Bonnie."

"Is she trying out?"

"No, she's helping with the publicity, but she saw the whole thing. Will you call her, Jerr-o? Ask her if I was really that bad?"

"Why don't you call her?"

"I can't. She'd just lie to keep from hurting my feelings. Please call her, Jerr-o."

Damn. Bonnie was the last person in the world I wanted to talk to. We'd had a brief meeting of the letters committee after school. No progress, just the same old arguments. "Is there anyone else I could call?"

"No. I want Bonnie's opinion."

I called the Tiger. "Hi, Bonnie. Jerry Kinkaid here."

"Why, Mr. Kinkaid. To what do I owe the pleasure?"

Bitch, I thought. "Sheila wanted me to ask you how she did at the tryouts."

Bonnie hesitated, and her voice lost its sarcasm. "Not so hot."

"How bad is that?"

"Well, if you really want the truth, she stunk up the place. She forgot most of her lines and recited what she did know like she was reading nursery rhymes."

"Oh, boy," I said. "This is going to be tough. She wants a part bad."

"If it's any consolation, all the other girls were pretty bad too. Armstrong gave them all hell and told them to study tonight. Sheila still has a chance if she can get it together by tomorrow."

"I don't know how she's going to do it. She just tightens up when she gets onstage. I can't understand it; she's a great actress offstage."

"I think it just happens to some people. How upset is she?"

"She was crying. More angry than anything, I think. I guess I'll just tell her to study hard and keep her hopes up. Thanks, Bonnie. I'll see you."

"Just a second. Let me think." For half a minute there was silence. "Call her back and tell her we're coming over. I live at 803 Riveredge. Pick me up."

"What are you going to do?"

"Nothing fancy. Just rehearse her. When can you get here?"

I almost asked her why she should give a damn about Sheila's success or failure, but I stopped myself. Anything she could do to help was going to make my life one hell of a lot easier.

I told Mom where I was going, turned down Melissa's offer to come along, and drove into town. Bonnie came out to the car, dressed in jeans and a lined denim coat. She had her hair back in a ponytail and looked a bit more human than usual. "Hi," she said. "Here's what we're going to do." She started describing her plan for getting Sheila over stage fright.

It worked. Bonnie started by getting Sheila to mimic how she'd screwed up that afternoon. The clown in Sheila came out, and she did a hilarious parody of herself. Then Bonnie had her go through the scene straight. I had the script and prompted her when she missed a line. Bonnie took her through the scene a half dozen times, making suggestions the first few times, then just letting Sheila get comfortable with it. Finally, she said, "O.k., Sheila, now just forget about it. You've got it down; you'll do fine."

Sheila sat. "Do you think I've still got a chance?"

"Sure," Bonnie said. "When you're not nervous, you're better than any of the others." I nodded my agreement.

"Thanks, guys. I feel a lot better." We heard the outside door open. "Granny's home. She was out playing canasta." Sheila got up and hurried into the kitchen. In a couple of minutes she was back, leading Mrs. Porter by the arm. "Granny, Bonnie and Jerry have been helping me rehearse for the play. Do you want to see me do the scene?"

Mrs. Porter smiled at us, but didn't say anything. She sat dutifully, and Sheila ran through the scene flawlessly. I glanced at Mrs. Porter a couple of times. She was a small, thin woman in her seventies with yellowish-white hair wrapped in a scarf. The few times I'd met her, she'd always looked tired and not quite with it. Now, I could see her attention wandering. Perhaps Sheila noticed too, but she didn't seem to mind. She'd told me before that "Granny gets distracted easy."

We applauded. Mrs. Porter got up, mumbling, "You kids must be hungry," and shuffled into the kitchen.

Sheila smiled at us. "Don't mind Granny. When she's tired she acts a little strange."

We sat around for half an hour drinking pop and eating cookies. Bonnie spent the time talking to Mrs. Porter. The old woman became positively animated about her card game. Bonnie smiled as if she was enjoying the conversation.

When we left, Sheila held me back at the door. "Thanks, Jerr-o. This helped a lot."

"It was Bonnie's idea."

"Ya, but you went along with it. Thanks, Steady." She kissed me. "And watch yourself on the way home. She may try to come on to you."

"Ya, sure. And I'm going to get drafted by a pro team tomorrow."

"I wouldn't be surprised." She kissed me again. "'Night, now."

A light snow was falling, and I took it easy as the streets started to slicken. After two or three blocks, I took a deep breath and said, "Thanks, Bonnie. I appreciate your help."

"I did it for Sheila, not for you."

Cripes, couldn't you say anything to the woman without getting snapped at? "Well, I know that. I'm just saying thank you too."

"You're welcome." She dug in her purse and found a package of cigarettes. "Mind?"

"Go ahead." She lit one. "I'm surprised you smoke."

"Now and then. Especially when I'm feeling lousy."

I hesitated. "What's the problem?"

She stared coldly at me. "Do you really want to know? It's because Sheila, for all her stumbling around, is going to pull it off. She's going to get a lead in that play and do a good job. But if I tried for a thousand years, there's no way I could do it. Just no way." She ground the cigarette into the ashtray. "And that significantly pisses me off."

"Then why did you help her?"

Bonnie shrugged. "She's a friend. I have to help the few I've got."

"I've always thought it was kind of odd you two were friends. You're not very much alike."

Confession time was over. "Don't try to psychoanalyze it, Kinkaid. You don't have the brains."

I was about to get mad, but then there was a thumping from the back of the car. Oh, shit. I pulled over and got out. The left rear tire was flat. Great. Just great. Bonnie came around for a look. "Well," she said brightly, "here's another fine mess you've gotten us into."

"Oh, shut up," I said. She laughed and leaned against a fender smoking another cigarette as I got out the jack and spare. I set the jack, brought the bumper up a couple of notches, then popped the hubcap and loosened the lug nuts a turn. What a goddamn time for this to happen. I returned to the jack and levered the car up until the tire was off the ground.

Bonnie watched. "Can I do anything?"

"Just stay out of the way." I pulled a couple of the nuts and started loosening the others, then hesitated. The car wasn't high enough yet. I went to the jack again.

"You know," Bonnie said, "the base of that jack is kind of at an angle."

I turned on her. "Look, Tiger. You may be one of the smartest kids in school, and I'm not. But, believe me, I have a fair idea about how to change a tire."

"Maybe you do, but—"

"Just can it, Tiger." I worked the jack up two more notches. On the third, I felt the jack start to go. The car wobbled, and I leaped back. The jack slashed by my fingers, and the car crashed to the pavement.

I stood looking at my car. The loosened rear wheel leaned in at a crazy angle. I half expected Bonnie to start laughing. Instead she said quietly, "Are you o.k.?"

I nodded, not looking at her, then took a deep breath and went to examine the damage. Two of the lugs had sheered off and a third broke away in my hand when I tested it. The last two wouldn't hold the spare securely. "We're screwed," I said. "We're not going anywhere, now."

She squatted beside me and looked. "Well, let's walk over to my place. Dad will give you a ride home."

"I can call Phil."

"Then you'll need to use the phone." She picked up the jack and put it in the trunk.

We didn't make any small talk on the walk to Bonnie's. I was furious with myself, furious with her, furious with the whole damn world. She wasn't stupid enough to say "I told you so."

Mr. Harper wouldn't hear of me calling anyone for help. We got in his car and, of course, he had to drive over for a look at the damage. He gave me a good-natured lecture on the proper technique for jacking up a car before finally driving me home. I rode in back while Bonnie sat with her father in the front. She didn't say anything, just stared at the night through the side window. I guess to make me feel better, Mr. Harper started telling stories of the troubles he'd had with cars over the years. I tried to sound interested. Bonnie put a hand over her mouth, and I could see her shoulders shaking. The bitch was laughing at me!

Her father's about six four and 240, so I couldn't kill her then, but I sure as hell felt like it. It was tough to be polite when I got out. I guess I pulled it off.

The next afternoon, Phil, Gary, and I talked our way out of sixth-period study hall and went to fix the car. Fortunately, the snow had melted and the sun was warm. Gary knew his way around cars best, so he did the surgery. He pulled the drum, hammered out the stubs of the three broken lugs, and drove in three new ones. We had the car fixed well before practice began.

Sheila's day was going better too. She called me in the early evening. "Jerr-o, I knocked them dead! I mean, I was dynamite!"

"You got the part then?"

"Not yet, but I know Armstrong's going to give it to me."

"Maybe you should be a little cautious."

"Cautious? Not this girl. I can see the future now. I'm going to be a star, and you can be my agent. I'll buy you a basketball team, and you can be a star too."

"I'm kind of short for the pros."

"Details. Details. Why are you always hung up on the details? Come over and pick me up. We're going to paint the water tower."

And, by God, she wasn't kidding. She had a can of paint and two brushes. "I'm going to paint S. LOVES J. in eight-foot letters right up there where everyone can see."

I told her that I didn't like high places, and, furthermore, that I didn't think we'd keep our illustrious positions at Conklin High after they caught us. I think my exact words were: "We could get in some deep and very serious shit." It

39

took quite a bit of convincing, but she finally recovered her sanity enough to agree to go out for hamburgers instead.

At the drive-in, she gave me a rundown of her triumph, concluding, "And it's all because you and Bonnie came over to rehearse me last night."

I grunted. "Ya, why do you suppose she went to the trouble?"

Sheila shrugged. "She's my friend, and she's got a big heart."

"Oh, bull. The Tiger's got a heart of stone."

"Jerr-o! She doesn't either. I told you how she tutored me in geometry last year."

"Your counselor set that up. Bonnie got extra credit."

"Well, so what? She was real patient, and since then she's been friendly. I mean, it's not like we're close, but we talk every once in a while. I think she's lonely. She doesn't have a lot of friends, and she's an only child, and her mother travels a lot on the job."

"Her parents probably decided one bad mistake was enough. Are you sure her mother doesn't travel just to get away from her?"

Sheila looked at me in exasperation. "Jerr-o, if I didn't know better, I'd say you were the one with the heart of stone. Maybe you don't like her, but I do. Now let's just forget about it before we get in a fight."

I shrugged. "Suits me."

When we got back to Sheila's, I thought the time might be right for a little heavy-duty groping. No luck. All I got was a quick kiss at the door and her usual excuse about needing her sleep. Well, I'd probably spoiled the mood by running down Bonnie. Still, sooner or later, Sheila was going to have to stop making excuses, or I'd have to start looking elsewhere.

As Bonnie had predicted, Sheila got the part. Sheila put

40

everything into the practices. I'd go down to the auditorium after basketball practice to see if she was unoccupied for a few minutes, but she'd be onstage rehearsing, studying the script, or running around helping with sets and costumes. Being ignored didn't sit real well with me at first, but I soon found myself enjoying the freedom. Hunting season was just around the corner, and I needed some time to get my gear together.

The gray, early light cast long shadows in the woods around me. After a few minutes, I could make out the far side of the clearing in front of my hunting stand. I shifted my weight to rest the rifle and my gloved hand against the tree trunk. I wanted to stamp my feet to warm them, but the snow was crusty, amplifying the sound of the slightest movement.

It was the weekend before Thanksgiving and the first morning of deer season. Gary, Phil, their fathers, and I had been in the woods since well before dawn, forming a ragged line along a network of deer trails running through a stand of hardwoods. The tension of waiting pumped adrenaline through my system until my senses sang in the sharp air.

Sheila and a lot of the people I knew couldn't understand what I was feeling in these minutes before the sun rose over the trees. Over hamburgers or steak dinners, they could denounce hunting without missing a bite. But death was no more cruel in the woods than the slaughterhouse. If I killed a deer this morning, it would put close to a hundred pounds of meat in the freezer—meat that we wouldn't have to buy with Mom's hard-earned wages.

Now Bonnie wouldn't be stupid enough to attack deer hunting as cruelty to animals. No, she'd say something about men reverting to savagery because of their discomfort with civilization. She'd snicker, use fancy words, and try to make us feel like we were throwbacks to the cavemen. I could almost hear her: "If you guys want all the primal benefits, why don't you throw away your rifles and use spears and clubs?" Well, she could go to hell too.

A buck stepped cautiously into the clearing. I started in spite of myself. He was big, six, maybe eight points, his thick neck still swollen from the rut. For long seconds, he waited for movement or the scent of man in the surrounding woods. Then he snorted and trotted out from the shadow of the trees. My motions were smooth, almost unconscious. The rifle snugged into my shoulder, and the cross hairs of the scope came down on the spot behind the forelegs where the heart lay beating beneath the tan hide. I barely felt the recoil or my right hand throwing the bolt up and back to eject the spent shell. The echo of the first shot had a dull sound, told me that the bullet had hit. The deer leaped, and I could see the red on his coat. I slammed the bolt forward and down, seating and locking a fresh shell in the chamber. My second shot broke the buck's neck, and he went down.

I put on the safety and walked the hundred feet to where the buck lay. He was beautiful, 160 or 170 pounds, far bigger than the two I'd shot previous seasons. I slit his throat with my knife and stood back. I was elated, but a little sadness tinged my emotion. He had been very beautiful alive. Ya, I told myself, but it's damn hard to eat them when they're still running around.

We had a basketball game that night and actually won for a change. Phil and Gary both had great nights, but the victory really belonged to Mike Bowker, who thoroughly unhinged their point guard. Mike was our ball hawk: tough, mean, and fast. Like a lot of Indian kids, he rarely said a lot or showed much emotion off the court, but I'd played ball with him long enough to know there was a hell of a lot more to Mike than he liked to let on. New kids at the school were surprised to find out that he was an A student and president of the Native Americans Club. Even people who'd known him for years often missed his wry jokes. We'd never been close, but I liked Mike and was happy that he was having a good night, even though it meant I rode the bench for all but about three minutes.

After the game, Sheila and I went out and slam-dunked some junk food. All she talked about was play practice. The cast had read through the play twice and would start working on individual scenes Sunday afternoon. She wanted to go home early to catch up on her sleep. "Jerr-o, I'm just so tired. I've had practice every night this week, and then I've had to do stuff around the house, then stay up late to do homework. It's not that I don't want to be with you, Steady; I'm just exhausted."

I was hurt, but shrugged my shoulders. "I could use some sleep too. It's going to be a real chore butchering that deer tomorrow."

"Ugh. Don't talk about that."

On the way to her house, she started complaining about the amount of homework she had to do. I listened with half my attention while I thought about the rest of the evening. Maybe I'd drive over to Junction and see what was happening at the Purple Horse. "And algebra. I can't understand that stuff. Why do they make us take it? I mean, when will I ever need to know algebra?"

"It might come in useful when you're making millions in the movies. Help you to keep track of your income and all that."

"I'll have an accountant to figure that stuff out. You can keep an eye on him, Steady." She gave my knee a squeeze.

"It doesn't sound like your plans give me much to do."

"Oh, you'll have lots to do. You'll be my manager, my agent, and my lover."

"Well, I can take on one of those roles any time you're ready."

"Do you think I need an agent now?"

"I was speaking of lover."

She snuggled close. "One of these days." She stuck her tongue in my ear, and I damn near hit a telephone pole.

I pushed her away as well as I could. "Keep doing that, and we won't live long enough."

She giggled, but then was serious. "Jerr-o, I'm going to flunk algebra if I don't get some back assignments in. Can you help me?"

"I guess. When?"

"How about tonight? I won't have time tomorrow."

I groaned inwardly. Doing algebra wasn't exactly my idea of excitement on a Saturday evening.

The house was a mess. It had never been overly clean or orderly, but it was considerably worse than usual. Sheila gathered the dirty dishes from the table and piled them precariously atop the stack in the sink. She got her algebra book, and we sat down. I worked a couple of problems for her, but I could see she wasn't paying much attention. "I'd better check on Granny."

She came back in, opened a can of soup, dumped it in a saucepan, and began to make a peanut butter sandwich. "She hasn't eaten. Go ahead and work on the assignment. I'll catch up."

"I don't know if that'll work so hot. You should do most of it yourself if you're going to pass the test."

"I said I'd catch up," she snapped. I shrugged and returned to the algebra. Sheila carried supper into her grandmother's bedroom, then came back to the kitchen and started the dishes. I finished the assignment and got up to

44

help her. "Why don't you stick to the algebra?" she said. "I'll do this."

"It's really not going to work, Sheila. You know and I know—"

She set down a cup so hard that the handle came away in her fingers. She looked at the semicircle of china in disgust, then turned to me. "Jerr-o, for Pete's sake, just don't lecture me tonight. I need to get those assignments in. I'll study for the test when the time comes. Just help me out a little, huh?" My face must have shown my surprise, then my rising anger. She reached out a hand and touched my cheek. "Please, Jerr-o?"

I worked fast after that. All I wanted to do was get done and get out. Maybe there'd be a girl at the Purple Horse who could be both civil and sane. That would be a nice change.

But I'd been up since before dawn and, by the time I finished Sheila's homework, I was too beat to think about anything except going home to bed. At the door, Sheila said, "Jerr-o, I love you. You know that, don't you?"

"Ya, sure."

"I do. I really do. Just help me get through this, huh?"

"Sure," I said, and I guess I meant it.

FOUR

Sheila came for supper the day before Thanksgiving. Melissa knew her a little from school, but Mom had only seen her briefly. Sheila was on her best behavior: smiling, cheerful, and not too loud. She asked questions, waited for the answers, and kept her own replies down to a reasonable length. The main course was almost over when Melissa asked Sheila about the play. That's when Sheila lost it. She stopped eating and started babbling.

After three or four minutes, I tried to slow her down, but just then she got it in her head to do a parody of Armstrong, the director. It was funny all right—Melissa was almost falling off her chair—but more than a little bizarre. I glanced at Mom. She was smiling, but I could tell she was a bit taken aback by Sheila's antics.

Suddenly, Sheila needed props. She jumped up and pulled her chair back to the middle of the room. "And see, we're going through this scene where I'm supposed to be up on a chair dusting a picture, and Mr. Henson, the villain, who really isn't a villain, but turns out to be the hero, comes in and surprises me. Here, Jerr-o, you be Mr. Henson."

"Ah, Sheila—"

"It's o.k., you don't have to do anything. Just go over there and make like you're coming in the door. Then say, 'Hello, Bridgette.'" Unwillingly, I got up and followed instructions. "Anyway, you see Armstrong's out in the audience watching—not yet, Jerr-o—and I'm up on the chair." She climbed up. "Now I'm really afraid of Mr. Henson, because I think he may be the murderer or at least knows something about the murder, which he does, but that's not important right now, so I've really got to show I'm frightened when he surprises me. O.k., now, Jerr-o."

I made like I was opening a door, took a couple of steps, and said, "Hello, Bridgette." Sheila gave a scream and jumped about three feet straight up. The scream was good enough to lend some excitement to the scene, but the jump really did it. As I've said, Sheila wasn't small, and when she came down her right foot went right through the cane seat of the chair. The chair and Sheila tumbled. There were exclamations from the audience and an "Oh, shit" from me.

Sheila rolled over on her back, the chair stuck to her leg. Embarrassment followed surprise, and she blushed crimson. I went to free her. "Are you hurt?" She bit her lip and shook her head. I managed to wiggle the chair off her leg.

"Well," Mom said, "that was quite a performance, Sheila. Jerry, get her another chair. Would anyone care for some pie?"

We got through the rest of the dinner o.k. Sheila didn't say anything for a long time, just sat with her head bowed, eating her pie mechanically. I could tell she was nearly in tears. She was quick to help clear the dishes. In the kitchen, I heard her say, "Mrs. Kinkaid, I'm so sorry. I'll pay for—"

48

Mom cut her off. "It's all right, dear. Don't worry. Jerry can fix the chair. I know young people get carried away with enthusiasm sometimes. I did when I was a girl. Now why don't you and Melissa start the dishes while I put the leftovers away."

On the ride back into town, Sheila sat quietly on the other side of the front seat. I thought I should say something about it being o.k., that I'd fix the chair and that Mom didn't hold grudges. But before I could start, Sheila turned to me. "You know, I bet we could do that during the play. We could weaken the seat just enough so it wouldn't break when I was standing on it, but when I jumped, *kerraash*, right through. Can you imagine, Jerr-o? Why, the audience would be absolutely convulsed! And then Henson could have a lot of trouble getting the chair off my leg, and I'd be worried about keeping my dress down, and afraid he was going to murder me. My God, by the time we got done, they'd have to bring in ambulances and stretcher-bearers to carry the audience away!"

That was my Sheila.

That evening, I took the broken chair to the basement and tried to figure out how the hell I really was going to fix it. Mom was doing some wash. "Well," she said, "Sheila certainly is a character."

"Ya, she's a lot of fun, Mom. She's real sorry about the chair."

"I know. It's partly my fault; I shouldn't have let her climb on it."

"It's kind of hard to get in a word with her sometimes."

Mom spent a minute separating clothes. "I don't want to pry, dear, but I'm a little surprised that you're attracted to a girl who's, well, pretty enough, but maybe a little empty-headed sometimes." She glanced at me to see how I was going to take that; it wasn't often she stuck her nose in my personal business. I didn't say anything. "It's just that I'd have thought you'd pick a girl with a more serious side."

"It's not as if we're going steady or anything, Mom."

"That's not what I heard from a couple of the women at the mill."

News gets around, I thought. "Well, Sheila was bugging me about it, so I said that she could say we were sort of going steady, but we haven't exchanged rings or anything."

Mom started the washer. "I see. Just be careful, dear. I'm not telling you not to have fun, but, well, just be careful."

"Don't worry, Mom. I'm not going to get trapped."

"That's good," she said, and went upstairs.

I knew that Mom had said a couple of pretty accurate things. Maybe I would have been happier with a girl who had a more serious side. There was no such thing as taking a quiet walk with Sheila or just sitting around having a more or less serious discussion. Still, I couldn't say I was unhappy. We had fun, and she made me laugh. She was more than "pretty enough"; she was one of the best-looking girls in the high school. And even if sex wasn't real high on her agenda, she liked me, even said she loved me, and that felt pretty damn good. Cripes, what was I complaining about? Give it a little time, Kinkaid. Hell, you've only been going out with her for three months.

I didn't have much time to worry about it anyway, since we were both busier than hell. With homework, play practice, basketball, and a dozen other things going, we weren't seeing a lot of each other.

The stupid letters thing constituted the biggest pain in my butt. The committee met again the week after Thanksgiving. The basketball team had gotten pounded in a holiday tournament over the weekend, so I was expecting a

couple of shots from Bonnie. Instead, she had a new pro-
posal: she wanted to poll the student body on the letters
issue. She'd even made up the ballot.

She passed out copies, and we examined it. "Cripes," Phil
said, "can you imagine how much work this is going to be?
It'll take days, weeks maybe."

"You're exaggerating," Bonnie said. "It won't be that
bad."

"I think it's a lousy idea," Phil said. "Even if one side does
win a clear majority, that's not going to make their opinion
right."

Some of the other kids joined in the discussion. As usual,
opinion was pretty much divided. After a few minutes,
Bonnie looked at me and asked, "What do you think?" In
her expression I thought I caught a hint of "You owe me
one, Kinkaid."

"Well, I don't think it would hurt. The wording could be
improved here and there, but I'm willing to go along with
the basic idea." For the first time since I'd known her, Bonnie actually smiled as if she meant it. And it was a nice smile.

We thrashed out some disagreements on the questions,
then voted. Seven to three. Progress.

The team left Friday afternoon for a weekend road trip to
the other side of the state. When Phil sat down next to me, I
noticed he had a good-sized hickey on his neck. "Who's the
lucky lady?" I asked.

"I'll tell you in a minute. Wait till we're rolling."

Coach Burke took the roll, then gave us a little lecture as
the bus pulled out of the parking lot: "Now, men, we
haven't been doing too well recently. As a matter of fact,
we've been making horses' asses of ourselves. I want to start
changing that right now. On this trip, we are going to
concentrate. We are going to think basketball, talk basket-

51

ball, play basketball, and live basketball. We're going to win, because we believe we're winners!"

"The jerk can't be talking about us," Phil muttered.

"Colburn, you got something to say?"

"Nothin' much, Coach. Just said, that's telling us, Coach. We believe!"

There were a few scattered cheers from the team. Burke didn't catch the sarcasm. Hell, we knew we were worse than mediocre. As Phil had once cracked, "Our lack of height is matched only by our lack of speed."

Things settled down. "So," I said, "who's the blood-sucker?"

Phil grinned. "A girl from over in Junction. Lisa Mac-Andrews. Know her?"

"I think someone pointed her out to me. Short blond with a gap between her front teeth, right? I was told she likes a good time."

"That's her, and she *definitely* likes a good time. She turned my eyeballs around three times last night."

I raised my eyebrows. "You don't say? Well, congrats."

He laughed. "Thanks. By the way, she's got a plan that might interest you. When she worked at Treblehook last summer, she discovered this smaller resort a couple of miles away where they don't ask too many questions or check IDs real close. She thinks we can get a couple of rooms cheap."

I glanced forward to see if anyone might be paying too much attention to our conversation. "Well, there goes training," I said.

"Screw training. This team wouldn't go anywhere if we all turned into saints. Do you think Sheila would go with you?"

"I don't know. Maybe. When is this supposed to happen?"

"The weekend after Christmas. We've got a game Friday night, but they're giving us Saturday off for a change."

"Sounds good. Oh, oh, Burke's going to talk B-ball."

Phil went crazy that night, and Gary was absolutely berserk. Phil had 19 and Gary 23 by early in the fourth quarter. I'd spelled Mike for a few minutes in the first half, but only had two points to show for it. The game had seven minutes to go when Mike got his fifth foul on a collision with their center. I pulled off my jacket, checked in, and joined Phil in the backcourt. He was panting and dripping sweat. "You're having a hell of a game," I said.

"Ya, and we are going to beat these bastards too. I'm sick of hearing crap from Burke. Here we go."

We won by 5, scoring more points than we had all season. Phil was sapped and fell asleep over the post-game supper. Maybe we weren't really winners, but at least we'd shut up Burke for one night.

We got pounded the next night—back to life as usual. Burke was seething on the way back, and I didn't blame him. We'd played a lousy game. It was going on midnight when we got into Conklin. Burke stood. "O.k., men, we had one good game and one piss-poor one. Let's practice hard Monday. Oleron will be in on Tuesday."

"Damn," Phil muttered. "I forgot about that Tuesday night game."

"Colburn, you got something to say?"

Phil didn't bother to lie. "I just said I'd forgotten about that game, Coach."

"Well, try to remember it and, while you're at it, try to remember how to run a fast break. That goes for the rest of you too."

For a second I thought Phil was going to explode, but he just tightened his lips. On the way to my car, he said, "If we don't get a new coach, I'm not going out next year. To hell with it. Cripes, my back is killing me."

"Maybe you ought to have Lisa walk on it."

Phil grinned. "Not a bad idea." He glanced at his watch. "She was going to waitress at a wedding party tonight. She gave me the number of the hall. I think I'll see if she's still there." He called from the pay phone across from the lot and got an answer. They talked for a couple of minutes, then he waved me over. He covered the mouthpiece with a hand. "She said the party's over, and she and another girl are cleaning up. They ripped off three bottles of champagne. Want to drive over and have some?"

"I don't know, Phil; it's pretty late."

"Hey, come on. You said your mom was working tonight. And if that other girl is a friend of Lisa's, you might score. Hell, you can't be getting much from Sheila these days."

I shrugged. "Suppose she's a dog?"

"Then all you've got to do is talk to her. Come on, give me a break, huh?"

"Ya, well, o.k."

"Good man."

We got to the Legion hall in Junction a little after midnight. I was still skeptical; this might not be very smart. When we got out of the car, Phil said, "Let me have the keys. Lisa and I might want to come out and listen to the radio." I grunted and handed them over.

Lisa let us in and hugged Phil. The other girl looked up from across the room. Oh, Lord, I thought. She was my height and probably as heavy. Not real fat, just big—the kind of girl who could throw haybales right along with the men. Maybe eat a couple too. She grinned and waved. "This is Maureen," Lisa said. "We've got beer and champagne. What do you guys want?"

"Beer," Phil said. "We'll save the champagne for later." I nodded.

We helped the girls clean the hall. When Phil and Lisa took some of the trash out, they didn't come back for a long time. Maureen smiled at me. "You guys are from the big town, huh?"

"If you mean Conklin, yes."

"That's big compared to Junction." She pushed a long table against the wall as if it weighed a few ounces. "I always wanted to go to school there, but it was just little Junction High for me."

"I guess they're talking about consolidating in a couple of years."

"What's that mean?"

"Putting the schools together."

"That'll come a little late for me. I graduated last year. Help me with this table, huh?"

"Sure. So what are you doing now?"

"Going to hairdresser's school. Want me to do yours?"

"Ah, no, thanks."

We got the last table out of the way. Maureen wiped sweat from her brow. "Whew. Well, I guess that does it. Let Lisa and what's-his-name sweep up when they get back. Me, I'm going to open one of those bottles of champagne."

I followed her into the kitchen where they had the champagne stashed. Maureen opened a bottle. "Come on, there's some kind of meeting room back here where we can sit down." She led the way down a hall and into a small room with a couch, some chairs, and a table. I was going to take one of the chairs, but she pulled me down next to her on the couch. She took a swig from the bottle and handed it to me, then lit a cigarette. "Want a smoke?"

"No, thanks."

"Ya, that's right. You're an athlete of some kind."

"Basketball." I handed her the bottle.

"I played some basketball in high school. They called me 'the Crusher.'" She grinned at me. "I'm five ten, one seventy. How about you?"

"Ah, five ten, one sixty."

55

She laughed. "I've got you by ten. Want to go one on one?"

"Ah, well . . ."

Out of the blue, she kissed me wetly. "Hey, relax. I know I ain't the trim beauty you might have been hoping for. Don't worry. Get a little drunk. I ain't going to rape you or anything."

I felt myself blush in the dim room. "It's not that, it's, ah—" She cut me off with a long kiss.

After some time and more of the champagne, it didn't seem so unnatural to be with her, and we got at it pretty good. Finally, she pushed me away and got up. She rebuttoned some of her clothing and lit a cigarette. "I'm going to get another bottle." When she came back, she handed it to me and sat down. I pulled her closer and slipped a hand under the side of her blouse. She kissed me briefly, then looked into my eyes for long seconds. "You got any rubbers, Jerry?"

"Ah, no."

"Too bad. I think I could make it with you." She leaned back against the opposite end of the couch. "But I don't take chances anymore. I was sorry once. I've got a kid at home." My face must have shown my surprise. She smiled ruefully. "Ya, Jerry, you are involved with an old and worldly woman."

She reached over for the bottle.

"The guy didn't marry you, huh?"

"Shit. That bum? I ain't seen him in over a year."

"I'm sorry."

"Ya, so am I." We heard laughter in the hall. "Well, I see the youngsters have screwed themselves silly." She got up. I followed. At the door she turned and kissed me. "It was nice, Jerry. If you get drunk enough, give me a call sometime."

"Sure," I said.

I called Sheila around noon on Sunday. I needed some cheering up; I was feeling both guilty and depressed. (My head didn't feel so hot either.) "Jerr-o, I can't talk now. Armstrong's holding play practice all afternoon. I'll call you later, Steady."

I watched the Packers while I finished fixing the chair Sheila had broken. Melissa came in, her coat and stocking hat white with snow, her fair skin pink from the cold. She sat down and changed film in her old camera. Photography was Melissa's passion, and she was always wandering the woods trying for pictures of birds and animals. "Hey, Jerry, I found a good Christmas tree down near the railroad tracks. Let's go cut it."

Good idea; I needed to get out. "O.k., give me a couple of minutes."

A feathery snow was falling, obscuring the hardwoods and the few tall pines along the edge of our property. We walked down through the long field that had been cleared long ago when this was a working farm. The field still grew a decent crop of hay, and a neighboring farmer cut it two or three times a summer. The snow was only about eight inches deep and the walking not bad. We traded off carrying the swede saw and dragging the toboggan. "You were out late," Melissa said. "Seeing Sheila?"

"No, the bus got back late. Then Phil and I ran into a couple of his friends."

"Anyone I know?"

"I doubt it. They're from out of town."

Melissa paused and trained her camera on the house through the haze of snow. She thought, then closed the case, and hurried to catch up. "I can't afford the film. I wish I could get a thirty-five millimeter. The film's cheaper and the camera's better. Maybe I'll ask Mom to spare me the sweaters and socks at Christmas so we can afford one."

"I thought girls were supposed to be more interested in clothes than cameras."

"When I'm a famous photographer, I'll be able to afford all the clothes I want. Maybe I'll work for *Playgirl*. Want to pose?"

"You should live so long."

"Well, they like taller, hairier guys anyway."

"How would you know?"

She grinned. "I've seen a few issues."

"Ya, well, hmmmm . . . Hey, where's that tree, anyway?"

"Over in the far corner. You can't see it yet. So, how's Sheila doing?"

"O.k., I think. I haven't seen her in a couple of days."

"I almost died when she went through the chair. God, that was funny. But kind of awful too. Does she still feel bad about it?"

"I think she got over it."

Melissa paused, then asked, "Are you and Sheila going steady?"

"She says so, I don't."

"Well, I think you should. I like her. She doesn't care what anyone thinks of her."

"Not very often."

There was another pause as Melissa searched for a topic that might get a decent conversation going. "You know Bonnie Harper pretty good, don't you?"

"Ya, I'm afraid so."

"You don't like her?"

"Not much."

"Well, I think she's kind of neat. She came into our social studies class last week and talked about Indian reservations and the medical problems a lot of Indian kids have. She made it pretty interesting. Did you know she's part Indian?"

"I suspected it."

"She wants to work on an Indian reservation as a nurse or something."

"Well, I guess she'll cure her patients or kill them. Is it one of those trees over there?"

"The one near the old gate. You can just make it out."

I was leaning over, tying the tree to the toboggan, when I felt a double handful of snow go down the back of my pants. I yelled and whirled to see Melissa racing for the house, the saw in one hand, her camera in the other. I got the snow out of my pants. Damn careless to turn my back on her. Well, I'd have my revenge later. I grinned nastily. Ya, make her worry about it, then get her with something really inventive when she was least expecting it.

That evening, we were decorating the tree when Sheila called. "How'd practice go?" I asked.

"O.k., but I'm just beat. And I've got stupid algebra to do. Can you come over and help me?"

This again. "Well, maybe, but we've got to make a deal this time. You've got to pay attention and do some of the problems on your own."

"Slave driver. O.k., it's a deal."

I drove over. Mrs. Porter had already gone to bed, so we had the living room to ourselves. Sheila curled up beside me on the couch as I spread her homework on the coffee table. She seemed to be concentrating for a while, but then she got a pillow, put it in my lap, and lay down. "You can't see like that," I said.

"Yes, I can. Go ahead. I'm watching."

I adjusted myself to the awkward position and started explaining factoring again. "Do you get it now?" She was asleep. I dropped the pencil and leaned back. Oh, hell. What should I do now? I shook her gently. She made a soft noise like a big cat purring and went on sleeping.

After a few minutes, I disentangled myself and tossed the blanket from the back of Mrs. Porter's chair over Sheila. I finished the algebra at the kitchen table and left a note: "Sheila, try to work through at least a couple of sample problems. See you tomorrow. Love, Jerry."

Burke was in a lousy mood at practice on Monday and laid into Mike Bowker for "lollygagging." Mike had started every game since the beginning of his junior year, and now Burke was threatening to bench him. Mike didn't utter a word, but I could see the hatred burning in his dark eyes. Phil was standing beside me. "Can you believe this shit?" he said. "Mike plays harder than any guy on the team."

Mike's silence drove Burke wild. He spun. "Kinkaid, you're starting tomorrow." I nodded.

Mike didn't show up to watch the JV game the next night. Everyone on the varsity noticed, but no one said anything. It figured; we all knew that you didn't treat Mike or any Indian that way. Hell, you didn't treat anyone that way. If one of us had gotten up at that point and said, "To hell with you, Coach, I quit," I think we all would have walked out.

During the second quarter, I went into the hall to get a drink from the fountain. Mike was there with Bonnie. "Mike, you can't quit," she was saying. "Think of what it would mean. How many Indian kids play varsity sports here?"

Mike was raging. "The hell I can't quit! That son of a bitch humiliated me in front of the whole team. And I can run the legs off any white kid around, but the goddamn white coach thinks he can dump all over me."

"He's a jerk. Everyone knows that. But you've got to think about the other Indian kids in the school. You're a source of pride for us."

"Since when were you Indian?"

"Well, I'm not very much, but I've got a little in me."

"Ya, right. A little. You don't know what it's really like. You don't know anything about working your ass off and then getting dumped on. Well, I do! And I'll tell you what *my* pride tells me to do. It tells me to quit playing a white man's game. Screw Burke and all the rest of them!"

Bonnie spotted me. "Kinkaid, come over here and tell Mike he can't quit."

Mike turned. "Hell, he's starting in my place tonight. He doesn't want me on the team."

"Mike, you know damn well that's not true," I snapped. His eyes challenged me: prove it. I took a deep breath. "Look, I don't know what you should do, but I don't think you should quit. Personally, I don't give a damn if you represent anything to the Indian kids in this school or not. But you're a hell of a good basketball player, and Burke's got no right to take that away from you." Mike stared at me for a long moment, then looked down, his lips tight. "You know he's not going to keep you on the bench for long, Mike."

"Come on, Mike," Bonnie said. "Jerry's right."

Mike took a step so he could look in at the court. "You want to play, don't you?" I asked.

He grimaced. "Ya, sure, I want to play. . . . For me and for some other reasons. But I've missed almost half the JV game, and I'll be damned if I'm going to apologize to Burke about it."

I thought fast. "Don't worry about that. Just get changed and come in the far door."

"Ya, and suppose Burke tells me to get lost."

"I'll walk out with you. And I think Phil, Gary, and most of the others will too."

Mike looked uncertain. Inside, the teams came downcourt fast. Tennis shoes squeaked on the hard floor, the basketball caromed off the rim, and a ref blew his whistle. "I've got to play," Mike said, and headed for the locker room.

I started back inside. "Jerry," Bonnie said. I turned to her. "Thanks, I appreciate it."

I gave her an answer I knew she'd recognize. "I did it for Mike, not for you, Tiger."

She nodded. "I guess I had that coming. Thanks anyway."

I sat down at the end of the row and told Phil what had happened. He raised his eyebrows. "Burke is going to tell him to shove off."

I shook my head. "Not if we do what I have in mind. Pass this down the line . . ."

When Mike came in and walked sullenly to where the team sat, we all stood and one by one reached for his hand. "Hey, Mike," Phil said, "we're gonna get these bastards."

"Get your war bonnet on, Chief," Gary said, and the other guys chipped in. Down at the end of the row, Burke looked surprised, then grim. He decided to ignore the whole thing—one of the few intelligent things I'd seen him do.

I had a good first half, but picked up my third personal at the start of the third quarter. Burke sent Mike in, and he'd never played better. He was like a cat, slashing out to steal the ball from an Oleron guard, pouncing on a ball that popped loose inside, gliding downcourt alert for an open man. But they were tough inside, and we trailed by one with twenty seconds to go and Oleron in a stall. Then Mike tomahawked the ball out of their point guard's hands, and he and Phil broke downcourt two-on-one against their other guard. Mike fed Phil for the winning basket, and Phil threw it right back to him. Mike swooped in, spun it off the glass, and we won. I could almost hear war drums pounding in Mike's heart.

He dressed beside me in the locker room. "That's a crummy belt you've got, Kinkaid. Here, trade." He handed me his tooled-leather belt with its beautiful silver and turquoise buckle.

"Mike, I couldn't—"

He put a finger to his lips. "Sshh. Old Indian custom. Don't mess with the medicine, white boy." He winked and pointed to my belt. I gave it to him.

FIVE

When Sheila didn't meet me outside the locker room, I figured that she was still at play practice. With only a week and a half before opening night, Armstrong was pushing the cast hard. Sheila was confident that she had her role down, but some of the others were struggling. Well, she'd know that most of the team would head for the bowling alley for pizza after the game. Maybe she'd get away in time to meet me there. Otherwise, I'd call her later.

We'd kept it down in the locker room, not laughing about how we'd rescued Mike from Burke, but once we were at the bowling alley, that was the main topic. We felt like a real team for a change. Maybe all that united us was our hatred of the coach, but it had worked. We'd played well and won.

The cheerleaders and a few of the kids from the pep band joined us. They knew something had happened, but weren't sure what. To my surprise—and probably everyone else's—Mike spoke before any of us could tell the story. "I got benched. The guys were just showing that they still had confidence in me. That's all there was to it." We all nodded agreement—better to keep the details in the family.

Sandy Evans, one of the cheerleaders, was sitting next to me, and we fell into conversation while most of the rest of the kids got ready to go home or bowl a quick line or two. I'd been friends with Sandy for a long time, and it was good to have a chance to talk. We'd been sitting by ourselves for maybe ten minutes when I felt a tap on my shoulder. I turned to see Sheila staring holes in us. "Let's go," she said.

"Don't you want something to eat or drink?"

"No. Come on."

I glanced at Sandy, shrugged, and stood up. "O.k. See you tomorrow, Sandy."

I was ticked, but so was Sheila. In the car, she got the first sentence out. "What was that all about?"

"What was what all about?"

"You having that little heart-to-heart with Sandy."

"It wasn't a heart-to-heart. We were talking. Is that a crime or something? And another thing, where do you get off ordering me around like that?"

She stared at me, and then suddenly there were tears in her eyes. "You were planning to cheat on me. I could tell by the way you were looking at her." She started to cry, head in her hands.

I groaned, then put a hand on her shoulder. "You're imagining things. Sandy and I are old friends. And besides, I think she's going with Jim Frieborg." Sheila continued to cry, and alarm bells started going off in my head. "Hey, is something else the matter?"

"I got kicked out of the play," she whispered.

"You what?"

"I got kicked out of the play!" she shouted. "Can't you hear, you dumb ass?" Then she was holding on to me and

66

really sobbing. Oh, Christ, I thought, what happened?

It was ten minutes before I could get her calmed down enough to tell the story. She'd been backstage looking for something to do while Armstrong was taking some of the other actors through a scene. She'd noticed that the trim on one of the sets wasn't painted. She called it a flat, and I gathered it was the fake wall of the drawing room where a lot of the action took place. She found some paint and a brush, and climbed a ladder to finish the job.

"I was going along just fine and really proud of myself because Armstrong is always bitching about people just sitting around and not looking for something to do and then . . ." She had to take a deep breath. "And then when I was leaning out to get the last corner, the stupid ladder tilted. I grabbed the top of the flat, but the dumb ladder just went right out from under me. And I've got hold of the top of the flat, and I just kind of swung in, and—" She couldn't finish.

"And went right through the flat," I said.

She nodded and took a choked breath. "And then I lost my grip and fell. I tore the whole flat all the way to the bottom. Just ruined it."

"Were you hurt?"

"I wish I'd been killed. The flat's only the start. The can of paint I'd been using lands on the stage and splatters the curtains. Everybody hears all the noise and sees the paint running out under the curtains. Lots of people come running backstage. Armstrong yells for someone to get a rag to wipe up the paint before it soaks into the stage. He asks if I'm hurt, and I tell him I'm o.k. Then he runs off to try to save the curtains. When I go over to help, he yells, 'Get away. You've done enough damage. Get out of my theater.'

"And, Jerr-o, my butt hurts, and I feel terrible, and I just don't know what to do, so I just kind of went a little crazy. I

67

started yelling at him that all I was trying to do was help. And that it's not my fault if he's too cheap to buy decent ladders. And that he can't kick me out of the show because where is he going to get another Bridgette? And he yells, 'We have understudies to replace idiots like you.'"

She pressed her face against my chest. "And I ran out. I blew it, Jerr-o. I tried so hard and I blew it. He's right, I'm just an idiot." She started crying hard again.

It took me a long time, but I finally convinced her that there was still hope. I'd talk to Armstrong and try to smooth things over. I've had him for sophomore English, and I thought he liked me o.k. She wasn't optimistic, but my plan was about all she had.

I didn't sleep worth a damn and got up early to take a long walk in the field. Cripes, between Sheila and her problems, and Burke and basketball, and all the other crap coming down these days, I was getting wound up like a damn spring. Well, first things first. Talk to Armstrong and try to save Sheila's butt. Then deal with the other things one at a time. At least there'd be no B-ball practice, and I could get out of school as soon as possible.

I was thinking about what I was going to say to Armstrong when I almost collided with Bonnie in the hall near the main office. Her arms were loaded with ballots on the letters issue. "Kinkaid, I just went—"

"For God's sake, not now, Tiger. I've got a few other things going on in my life besides the damn letters thing." I left her standing there.

I checked Armstrong's schedule. He had first hour off. Good, I could talk my way out of chemistry lab for a few minutes without any problem.

I found Armstrong in the teachers' lounge. He had his feet up on a chair and was leaning back correcting a stack of themes. He looked tired, and his beard and dark hair seemed to droop. I knocked on the half-open door. He looked up. "Hi, Jerry. What can I do for you?"

"Ah, Mr. Armstrong, it's about Sheila Porter."

His eyes hardened. "Yes, what about her?"

"I heard about what happened last night, Mr. Armstrong. About the flat and the paint, and I, ah, know you had reason to kick her off the show. And she knows it too. But this play is really important to her, Mr. Armstrong, and, if there is some way to let her back on, I know she won't give you any more trouble."

He set his papers on the table and folded his hands in his lap. "So, why doesn't she come to see me? I hardly think it's an act of courage to send her boyfriend."

I hesitated. "She's scared, I guess. Scared and sorry and, ah, just very embarrassed." I felt my tone turn pleading. "Please, Mr. Armstrong, give her another chance."

He sat staring at me, then grunted and dug a pipe out of a suitcoat pocket. He spent a long minute filling and lighting it. "Miss Porter seems to have a growing fan club. You're the second person who's talked to me this morning."

"Who was the other?"

"Bonnie Harper. She made Sheila's case better than you have." I flushed. "I'll tell you the same thing I told her: If Sheila makes a ladylike apology to me, the cast, and the crew, I'll give her another chance. But in the future she had better think a little before taking on any project she doesn't understand." He raised a finger in warning. "And if she ever loses her temper like that again, I'll kick her tail so hard she'll never forget it." He paused. "That's the deal."

I nodded. "Thanks, Mr. Armstrong. I'll tell her."

I was just about out the door when he said, "Jerry, one more thing. Has Sheila been feeling all right recently?"

"How do you mean?"

"Mentally, physically."

"Well, I think she feels o.k. physically. She's just kind of tired and on edge, I think."

He nodded and picked up the pile of themes. I thanked him again and went back to chemistry. I'd catch Sheila between classes. I'd also have to find Bonnie sometime and say I was sorry for snapping at her. Damn.

When I apologized to Bonnie, she gave me a curt nod, but no crap about "I did it for Sheila."

At noon, I got Sheila out to my car and told her what Armstrong had said. She was still pretty down and embarrassed as hell, but she'd do anything to get back in the show. "Don't make a big deal out of it," I told her. "Stand up, say you're sorry, and sit down. That'll be enough." She bit her lower lip and nodded.

"Look, Sheila, after the play's over, let's get out of town for a couple of days. Phil and Lisa are going up north the weekend after Christmas. Lisa knows a resort where they rent rooms no-questions-asked. Let's go with them." Sheila didn't look at me. "Sheila, it'd be something to look forward to, a chance to celebrate after all the strain."

She leaned against me and put her head on my shoulder. She seemed about to cry again. "I'm not sure I could."

I could take that a couple of different ways. "Sure, you could. You could tell your grandmother you were going with some girlfriends."

She didn't say anything for a minute. "It'd really mean a lot to you, wouldn't it?"

"Well, we'd have fun, Sheila. You know, get away from Conklin, do some skiing, party a little, have a chance to be together. . . . Just think about it, huh?"

"O.k." She gave me a sad, soft kiss.

A lull came in my life. Sheila apologized and got back in the show. I studied and played basketball. Bonnie ran her letters survey, but it didn't prove much, since opinion in the student body was just about evenly split. Everyone on the committee—even Bonnie—said to hell with it at that point; we'd try to come to an agreement after the holidays.

Sheila didn't bounce back as fast as I'd expected. The memory of the great flat-painting disaster seemed to stick with her. She worked like hell getting ready for the play, but some of her earlier enthusiasm was gone. Around me, she was by turns snappish and apologetic. By unspoken agreement, we didn't see much of each other.

The play opened the Friday before Christmas. We had a road game, so I missed Sheila's debut. I talked to her Saturday morning, and she seemed to feel it had gone all right. That night, Mom, Melissa, and I went to the play. Sheila was good, maybe not quite as good as I'd expected her to be, but better than most of the others.

Mom and Melissa got a ride home with a neighbor, and I waited for Sheila. When she met me outside, I told her she'd been great. "Was I really? I mean, don't lie to me, Jerr-o."

"I'm not. You were good. Very good."

"Did the chair thing work?"

"It was the high point of the play. Mom almost busted a gut."

She laughed and took my arm. "Take me out for a hamburger. I haven't been able to eat all day. Then you can take me home to bed."

"Really?" We got in the car.

"Yep. Armstrong says no partying and no hangovers. He says there are understudies just dying for a chance at the leads. So I'm afraid it's going to be a quick date tonight."

"I thought you said something about me taking you home to bed."

71

"Huh? Oh, I get it." She grinned. "Must have been a fraudulent slip."

"Fraudulent? By any chance do you mean Freudian slip?"

"I'm not sweating the details." She laid a long kiss on me. We both came away a little breathless. She smiled. "You wouldn't want to wear out this star of stage, screen, and radio, would you?"

"Just give me the chance."

"Maybe next time. Come on, Steady. I'm starved."

I stood in the back of the theater for the last act of the Sunday afternoon performance. Sheila was cutting loose. She was twice as good as she'd been the night before. At the curtain call, she got the biggest round of applause. I was proud of her and more than a little relieved that it was all over. Better times were coming . . . at least I hoped so.

I helped strike the sets after the play. Armstrong's rule was that everything had to be cleaned up before any celebration began. It took all evening. About ten o'clock I went to the pop machine in the cafeteria. Bonnie and Bev Knutson were at a table counting receipts. I was still feeling good about all the species, even Bonnie. "How'd you come out?" I asked.

She waved a hand without looking up. "Hush, I'm counting." I got my pop and sat down nearby. Bonnie sighed and said to Bev, "Well, it's come out the same three times in a row. Somebody screwed up and we're six bucks short. I guess the program can stand it. You might as well take the cash boxes to Armstrong." Bev left. Bonnie leaned back. "Well," she said, "shall we try to have a civil conversation or should we just snap at each other?"

"Why don't we try the first? We can always move on if it doesn't work."

"Suits me. . . . Sheila was good this afternoon."

"Ya, I thought so too."

She studied me. "Mind if I ask you a question?"

"Go ahead, but I'm not promising any answers."

"That night you drove me home from Sheila's, you asked why we were friends. I'm going to ask you the same thing: Why do you two go out together? Somehow you don't seem very well matched."

I shrugged. "Everybody seems to say that. We have fun together, that's all the reason I've got."

She nodded. "That's a good one, I guess." She seemed to be thinking for a minute. Then she leaned back and stretched, her blouse coming tight across her breasts. Not bad, Tiger, I thought; you ought to do that more often. "I'm beat," she said. "I was at the hospital late last night."

"Why?"

She shrugged. "Oh, there's this old lady. She's dying, and I guess she wanted to talk. I listened."

"That was nice of you."

"Well, it was something to do on a Saturday night." She rose. "I'll see you in January. Merry Christmas." She pulled on her coat.

"Aren't you going to stick around for the cast party?"

Her tone was suddenly bitter. "No, they're all going to be obnoxious. Just wait and see. They'll spend hours congratulating each other while peons like us are ignored. I don't need that crap. Screw it."

The Tiger was back, but I asked a question anyway. "Then why did you work on the publicity?"

"Why? Because I wanted to see how good I'd be at it. Now that they've had the best attendance in years, I can pat myself on the back. If anyone thanks me, that'll be nice, but I don't need it. I know I did a hell of a good job, that's enough." She stared at me. "That doesn't make a damn bit of sense to you, does it, Kinkaid? Things come easy to you.

Like having fun. Some of the rest of us have to get off on other things. . . . Well, have a good time with the prima donnas. I'm going home."

She walked out, her boots making a lonely sound in the empty cafeteria. And the Tiger herself looked lonely—proud, but also small and vulnerable. I shook my head. Well, I wasn't going to let her spoil my good mood. If she was always uptight and bitter, that was her problem, not mine. I finished my Coke and smiled. It must be nearly party time.

At first I didn't want to believe that Bonnie had predicted the mood of the cast party so well. But she had. Anyone who hadn't been onstage was virtually ignored. The backstage people seemed to accept it and got in their own group. The few of us who were just along because we were going with one of the cast or crew members got left out. We hung on the edge of conversations and smiled a lot.

The party moved on from the backstage area around midnight. By two-thirty we'd hit three smaller parties at private houses. I was drained, but Sheila was in her glory. At three I gave up any idea of having even a few minutes alone with her. I got her away from another high-volume conversation and pulled her into the kitchen. "I'll be right back," she yelled as I closed the door. "What is it, Steady? Tell me quick, I don't want to miss this."

"I've got to go," I said. "Can you find a ride home?"

"Sure. I'll see you tomorrow, huh?"

"You're forgetting. Mom, Melissa, and I are going to my aunt's in Red Wing for Christmas. I'll see you on the twenty-sixth."

"Oh, Jerr-o, it went clean out of my head. I'm sorry. It's just all this excitement." She hugged me. "I'll miss you."

"I'll miss you too." I pulled back to look at her. "You haven't forgotten next weekend, have you?" She shook her head. "Will you go?" She hesitated, then nodded. "Overnight?" She nodded.

Someone yelled from the next room, "Hey, Sheila, you ought to hear this."

"Be there in a minute," she called, then turned back to me. "Good-bye, Steady. I'll see you in a few days. Merry Christmas." She kissed me.

For years we'd spent Christmas with Aunt Fran, Uncle Jim, and their twin girls, a year younger than Melissa. Mom and Melissa always looked forward to the trip, but the visits bored me. Fortunately, there was a cross-country ski trail not far away, and I got out every day.

The day after Christmas, we had the first blizzard of the season, so we laid over another day. I spent most of the afternoon helping Melissa figure out the manual for her new 35mm camera. The roads weren't clear until almost noon on Friday, and we didn't roll into our driveway until nearly dark. I grabbed a bite and drove in to school for the game. Burke started Mike, and I warmed the bench for the first three quarters, but got in for most of the fourth. We played better than average, but they whipped us on the boards and beat us by 8.

Afterward, a bunch of us met at the bowling alley. Phil had Lisa with him, and they acted like they were ready to crawl in each other's shorts right at the table. I was a little worried that Lisa might let slip a comment about my brief encounter with Maureen, but she didn't.

I was having a good time, and it irked me when Sheila nudged me and whispered, "Let's go home."

"What's the matter?" I asked. "You never used to quit early."

"I'm just tired. Please, let's go." I shrugged, and we got up.

"See you bright and early," Phil said and winked.

On the ride to Sheila's, I made a couple of cheerful comments about the trip, but got no response. Finally, she said, "I don't know, Jerr-o. Maybe we ought to stay in town."

I felt a jolt of surprise, then anger. After a moment, I said evenly, "I thought we'd agreed."

"Well, I'll go if it really means a lot to you, but don't we have fun here?"

Damn. Did we have to dance around the subject again? "Sure we have fun here, but this is our chance to get away and do something different."

She nodded. "I guess."

I put my arm around her, something I don't like to do when I'm driving. "Come on. You're just tired. We'll have a great time." She snuggled in, but didn't say anything.

When I turned the corner into Sheila's street the next morning, my insides were knotted tight. If she had a traveling bag, we'd be o.k. If she just had an excuse . . . Well, that'd be the end of things for us. I didn't even have my car parked when she dashed through the door with a small suitcase. She hopped in the car. "Quick, Granny's calling the cops! We've only got minutes to get out of town. Do you have the ring? How are we going to get our blood tests? Where's the preacher's? Come on, Steady, roll this crate!"

I dropped it in gear and slid the car away from the curb. "You are," I said deliberately, "nuts. Absolutely bats."

She grinned. "Only about you, Steady."

"How'd your grandmother really take it?"

"Oh, fine. I told her there'd be lots of kids and a couple of adult supervisors. Heck, I could enlist in the Marines and Granny wouldn't say boo."

We picked up Phil and Lisa and had a hilarious drive north. With all our baggage, we had a tight fit, and Sheila

76

got it in her head to do a sardine imitation. It was wild and weird: "And when we get there, they'll have to get out that long key from under the car. You know, it's just like the ones they have on sardine cans, but *muuucch* bigger. And they'll start at the front of the hood and peel the car back. And we'll be staring out through the windshield with our sad little sardine eyes. And—"

"This girl is crazy!" Phil yelled. "Jesus, stop, Sheila, my brain's curdling with the madness." Sheila, of course, poured it on.

We got to Saunders' Resort late in the morning. It was a little seedy, but at least there weren't a lot of people around. Registration went off without a hitch. We went to the bar and had no problem there either.

After lunch we drove over to Treblehook and skied for the rest of the afternoon. The temperature was perfect, the sky cloudless, and the slopes covered with six inches of new powder. Lisa fell down a lot, but the rest of us had good runs. God, Sheila was beautiful with her blond hair streaming behind as we rocketed downhill.

It was getting dark when we finished our last run and trooped into the lodge. I put my arm around Sheila. "I haven't seen a more beautiful girl on the slopes all day."

She smiled, but only weakly. "Thanks. I've got to go to the bathroom. I'll meet you in the bar."

The three of us found a table. Phil glanced toward the bar. "Well, no harm in trying." He came back with four beers. "Hey," he said, "things are loose in the north."

We drank the beer and got another round. Sheila had been gone a long time. Lisa said, "Maybe I'd better go check on Sheila. Need to drain off some of this beer anyway." She was back in a few minutes, looking worried. "She feels sick to her stomach. She said she'll be all right in a little while."

"Maybe she's just hungry," Phil said. "Let's get something to eat."

Sheila looked pale when she came in, but tried to smile. We ordered hamburgers, and the meal seemed to pick her up some. After supper, we got our suits from the car, changed, and tried out the pool. Phil and Lisa did a lot of giggling and wrestling with each other. Sheila spent most of her time sitting on the edge. I'd never seen her in a bathing suit before, and I appreciated her figure more than ever. Oddly, though, she seemed thinner than I'd expected.

I did a few laps, stretching the muscles and thinking. What was bothering her? Nerves? Or flu? Or had she just been hungry? I levered myself out of the pool to sit by her. "Want to try the Jacuzzi?" I asked.

"Sure."

We slipped into the hot, frothing water. Sheila sighed and closed her eyes. "When I'm rich, I'm going to have one of these. Maybe even a portable model I can take on location when I'm starring in a picture."

"You'll need a pretty big truck to move it."

"Details," she murmured.

"Are you feeling better now?"

"Oh, I feel o.k. Just relaxing."

"Have you lost a little weight?"

"I think so. I haven't had much time to eat these last few weeks."

"They've been a bitch, haven't they?"

She nodded. "But I wouldn't trade them, Jerr-o. Did you hear those people clapping for me after the last performance?"

"Sure did. You were the star."

"Ya, they loved me." She seemed almost asleep.

We sat close together, half suspended in the hot water. Relax, I told myself. She's o.k. Things are going to be fine. Ya, very fine. Suddenly, Sheila sat bolt upright and yelled,

"Hot! Let me out of here!" She jumped up, using a hand on top of my head to get her balance and dunking me good in the process. Then giggling and yelping, "Hot! Hot!" she dashed across the floor to the pool, nearly slipped, caught her balance, and dived in. She splashed Phil and Lisa and yelled for me to join her. Some of the older folks around the pool laughed and pointed out the obviously crazy girl.

After a few minutes of splashing around, she announced she wanted to go dancing. And when I say announced, that's exactly what I mean. Everyone around the pool heard her.

We changed again, then danced and drank beer until past ten. Phil and Lisa were getting pretty antsy by that time. I finally convinced Sheila to leave, and we drove back to Saunders' Resort. The manager let us buy a bottle of rum and some Cokes at the bar. On the stairs, Sheila said, "Come into our room, guys; we'll have a drink." Phil and Lisa glanced at each other, but followed.

Sheila turned on the TV and plopped down on the couch. Phil and Lisa sat on the edge of the bed. "We could play a game," Sheila said.

"We don't have cards," Phil said.

"Details. Charades is more fun."

"That's because you're an actress," Phil said. "I can't stand it."

"I'm not very good at it either," Lisa said.

They were distracted for a minute by something on the TV. I leaned over and whispered to Sheila, "For God's sake, can't you see they want to go to bed? If we don't let them, they'll go at it right here in about two minutes." She shrugged and looked a little hurt.

Phil set down his glass. "Well, I'm tired."

"Me too," Lisa said and hopped up.

We heard them giggling as Phil fumbled for the key to the room across the hall. "Want another drink?" I asked.

Sheila shook her head and stared at the movie on TV.

I got myself a drink, then sat beside her. She seemed engrossed in the movie. When I tried to pull her closer, she shrugged away. "I'm watching this part." I sighed and watched with her. The movie was exceptionally stupid. I tried again in a few minutes. "Darn it, Jerr-o. I'm watching a great actress."

"Who is it?"

"Katharine Hepburn."

"The hell it is. That's somebody else. Maureen something."

"Details. She's still good."

I got up and went to the bathroom, washed up, and brushed my teeth. I came back with only my jeans on and lay on the bed. Maybe she'd get the hint. After ten minutes, I lost patience. I sat up and crossed my legs under me. "Sheila, for cripes sake, are you going to watch that all night?"

She shrugged. "Maybe, it's pretty good."

"Well, come here then. You can watch it from bed just as easy."

She looked at me, and there were tears in her eyes. "I'm not going to do it, Jerr-o. I'm not going to make love to you."

I ran a hand through my hair. Steady, Kinkaid. Don't yell at her, or you'll spoil everything. I looked at her. She'd stretched out on the couch with her head on a pillow. She was staring at the TV as tears slowly slid down her cheeks. "Sheila," I said carefully, "it's o.k. if you're kind of scared. I mean, except for a couple of times before I knew you, I haven't done it either. Just come over here, and we'll hug for a while and see how it goes. You won't have to do anything you don't want to."

"I just can't. I just don't feel very good." I closed my eyes and sighed. Then she said something that made me open them like I'd been doused with cold water. "I haven't had my period in two months." I gawked. She didn't look at me. "And it's not because of what you're thinking. It just hasn't come."

Was I being bullshitted? Was she lying about not having her period? Or had there been some other guy? "Well, then how . . ." I paused. What the hell was going on? "Maybe it's just nerves or something."

"I don't know, but I just don't feel like doing anything."

I sat for long minutes, thinking. Finally, I turned off the bedside lamp and lay in the dark. Sheila stayed on the couch, her face ghostly in the light from the TV. After a while, I slept.

Long afterward I felt her slide in next to me. I came awake and lay aware of her long body inches from mine. I pressed in close and put my arm across her chest. She pushed my hand away from her breast. "Just hug me, Jerr-o."

After a minute, I asked, "Are you going to see a doctor?"

"Maybe next week." She paused, and I knew she was still crying. "Jerr-o, I love you. We'll do it sometime soon. Just let me get myself together a little."

But I didn't believe her. I lay there feeling lonely, confused, and hurt. And I knew she felt just as lousy, but I couldn't do anything about it.

I don't think she slept much. I'm sure that Phil and Lisa didn't. The three of them slept most of the way back to Conklin. I drove south along the narrow blacktop roads flanked by high snowbanks and leafless trees. I knew that Sheila and I were finished. And it wasn't just because she hadn't made love to me. Somehow we just weren't very happy together anymore. Ya, it was over. All we had to do was make it official.

I had no idea what a bitch that would be.

81

SIX

The water in the toilet was dark red with blood. My stomach lurched, and bile seared my throat. I fought it down and searched frantically for a clean towel. In the next room, Sheila sobbed and called for me. I kicked two or three bloody towels into a corner and found a clean one in the cabinet below the sink. I ran to her.

Sheila was lying on the couch, holding a bloody towel between her legs. "Here." I shoved it at her.

"I can't go like this."

"I'll get your raincoat." I ran to the hall closet. Blood stained the rug in front of the door where she'd collapsed after phoning me twenty minutes before. I'd answered to hear Sheila crying and gasping, "Jerr-o, I'm bleeding. I thought it was my period, but there's something wrong. There's so much of it. It's just gushing out."

"Sheila, calm down. Maybe, it's just . . . I don't know. Maybe you should call an ambulance."

"No, come here. Please." I heard her drop the phone.

"Sheila!"

"It's o.k. I'm back." She made an attempt to get control. "Just please come here, Jerr-o."

I moved, and it was damned fortunate no cop clocked my speed on the way into town. Sheila was lying just inside the door, conscious, but woozy. Her jeans and underwear were down around her knees, and the towel between her legs was soaked with blood. I picked her up and carried her to the couch, then ran to the bathroom for the clean towel.

Sheila was trying to pull up her jeans with the wadded towel in the crotch when I got back to the living room with her raincoat. It wasn't going to work. And neither was the raincoat. "Forget it, Sheila. We've got to get you to the hospital." I grabbed the blanket that always lay over the back of Mrs. Porter's chair, wrapped Sheila in it, and scooped her up.

"Granny," she said. "We've got to leave her a note."

"I'll call her from the hospital."

"No. Not with all this blood around."

Shit. Sheila was right. "O.k." I laid her back on the couch, found a pad and pencil, and scribbled, "Mrs. P., Don't worry. It's not as bad as it looks. I'll call from the hospital. Jerry Kinkaid."

I drove as fast as I dared to the emergency room, pulled to a hard stop at the door, and blew the horn. Cripes, would anyone hear? "I'll be right back." I jumped out to run inside.

A nurse and an orderly with a wheelchair hurried through the doors. "Where are you hurt?" the nurse demanded, pointing to my pants.

I glanced down; my coat and jeans were streaked with blood. "Not me, the girl in the backseat. She's bleeding from the . . ." What the hell was the word? "The, ah, you know, female organs."

"How much blood?" she snapped.

"Lots."

They didn't pay me any more attention. They had Sheila out of the car, in the wheelchair, and covered with a blanket in less than a minute. A minute later I was standing alone in the middle of the waiting room, staring at the closed doors of the examining room. I realized that I was acting like a punch-drunk fighter, wobbly and sticky with blood. I spotted the door to the rest room and went in. I was a mess; there was even blood on my face. I washed up as well as I could. Back in the waiting room, I laid a magazine across my lap to hide the blood on my pants.

Fifteen minutes passed before the nurse came back through the doors. I couldn't tell anything from her expression. "Come this way, please," she said. She led me into an office and told me to sit. "We've got the bleeding stopped for the moment. She lost quite a bit of blood, so we're giving her some fluids."

"Is she going to be all right?"

"We'll have to find the cause of the bleeding before we'll have any real answers. We'll be doing some lab tests in the next hour, and then the doctor will re-examine her. Now, I need some information from you. Were you having sexual intercourse when the bleeding began?"

"No! I mean, we never have."

She stared at me coolly. "You don't have to hide anything. We need correct answers so we can give her the best treatment."

I felt myself blush, half in embarrassment, half in anger. "I told you the truth. We haven't."

"She told us that she skipped her last period. Did she tell you that?"

"Yes, but she said there wasn't a chance of her being pregnant."

"And there isn't?"

"No, damn it, there isn't. . . . At least not with me."

The nurse nodded. "All right. She told us the same thing. We'll believe you."

"Thanks."

She ignored the sarcasm. "Since Sheila is a minor, we must have the consent of her guardian before we can treat her further. She said her grandmother is probably at the senior citizens' center but doesn't have a car. Can you pick her up?"

"I guess, but I . . . Hell, what am I supposed to say?"

For the first time, she seemed to show a hint of sympathy. "I'll call and talk to her. Just pick her up and tell her what happened if she asks."

I nodded. "Ya, o.k."

Sheila's grandmother was waiting just inside the door of the senior citizens' center. I got her in the car and started the drive back, intensely conscious of the dried blood on my coat and pants. "Mr. Porter used to get nosebleeds too," she said.

I stared at her in horror. "But, Mrs. Porter . . ." I dropped it.

She looked at me expectantly for a moment, then went on. "I remember when Phyllis, Sheila's mother, was a little girl she bumped Mr. Porter's nose and it started to bleed very hard. It took me an hour to get the bleeding stopped with ice packs. I wonder if they still use ice packs."

"Ah, I don't know. I guess you'll have to ask."

She rattled on about how Sheila's mother had been a bouncy kid and always roughhousing with Mr. Porter, but that on Sunday you'd never guess what a little tomboy she was during the week because she'd sit so nice and quiet in church and always looked so nice in the pretty dresses that Mrs. Porter made for her. "I'd like to make some dresses for

Sheila, but she doesn't seem to like anything but jeans. But maybe that's just as well. The arthritis in my fingers gets so bad sometimes that I can't even shuffle cards, and one of the other ladies has to do it for me. And I used to be so good at it. I could take two decks of canasta cards and . . ."

Jesus, I thought. What are they going to think of her at the hospital? Poor Sheila.

I sat in the waiting room while Mrs. Porter went in for a conference with the doctor. When she came out, she smiled at me brightly. "We can go now. They say Sheila's asleep, and they'll call when they know more. I told them I'll be at Cynthia Horner's. We're going to play poker." She giggled as if poker was something a little wicked. "It's a tradition with us on New Year's Eve."

New Year's Eve. I'd forgotten. This was the night I'd planned to break up with Sheila. I'd been thinking about how to do it since we'd returned from skiing a couple of days before. When I'd asked Phil's advice, he'd shrugged. "Tell her it's been fun, but you're in the mood for change. Then get out quick. And don't kiss her good-bye. That's asking for trouble." His technique sounded pretty brutal, but it made some sense. But now? Christ, what was I in for?

It was already late afternoon, and Mrs. Porter wanted to go directly to Mrs. Horner's. I dropped her off, then drove home. I'd go back to see Sheila in the evening. First, I had to change clothes. The memory of all the bloody towels in Sheila's house bothered me, brought the bile again to my throat. Should I go back and clean them up? The door was probably unlocked, but what would the neighbors think if I were in the house without Sheila or her grandmother around? To hell with it. Maybe the sight of the towels would wake the old lady up.

I wanted to talk to Mom about what had happened, but she'd grabbed the chance to earn double time on New

87

Year's Eve and wouldn't be home until morning. Melissa was gone too. She'd left a note on the kitchen table: "Dear Big Brother, Thanks so much for forgetting to take me to the slumber party. Fortunately, I wasn't raped or robbed while at home alone. Passing gypsies offered me a lift into town. Love, your darling sister. P.S. Don't worry your pointy little head about picking me up in the morning. Mom's stopping by on her way home from work." The note was topped with a drawing of a round face with a protruding tongue.

Damn. Well, she'd understand my forgetfulness when I explained. I thought of calling her, but decided against it. I didn't want to start the rumor mill grinding about Sheila.

In the shower, I started to feel better. I considered calling Phil. But, hell, he'd be partying already. I dressed and tried him anyway. I'd guessed right. I thought for a moment, then looked up Bonnie's number. I dialed the first five digits, then hung up. No, the Tiger might start asking the same questions the nurse had.

The night was clear and chill, the sky bright with stars. I drove slowly back to the hospital, giving myself time to think. I was probably making a big deal out of nothing. Sheila had missed a period or two and then something in that mysterious interior world of female organs had cut loose with a gusher of blood. They'd probably keep her overnight, then send her home in the morning. Hell, in a couple of days she'd probably have a new routine to describe our frantic rush to the hospital. Ya, she'd be o.k. Maybe she'd even tell me to hit a couple of parties tonight so I could tell her the gossip later.

The clerk in Emergency told me they'd moved Sheila to a room on the third floor. I went up. A nurse directed me to the room. "Just five minutes and be very quiet," she told me.

Sheila was lying with her eyes closed, her face very pale. They'd bunched her long blond hair under a blue cap, and IV lines ran from two bottles to a needle in her arm. I sat down beside her. She opened her eyes for a second, then closed them. She moved a hand in my direction, and I took it. "Hi, Jerr-o."

"Hi. You sure picked a strange way to spend New Year's Eve."

She smiled faintly. "Ya, bring in the New Year with a big performance."

"It was pretty dramatic."

"Ya, a real horror show. I'm sorry, Steady. It must have been awful for you."

"Don't worry about it."

She tried to grin. "Well, I finally let you in my pants."

"I guess so. . . . They asked me some questions about, you know, if we'd been at it."

"Me too. They didn't believe me at first."

"Me neither. Well, I guess they've got to find out those things."

"Jerr-o, I wish . . ." She started to cry.

"Hey, don't get upset. Everything will be o.k." She nodded, biting her lower lip. We didn't say anything for a couple of minutes. The nurse looked in and pointed to her watch. "The nurse is telling me I've got to leave. They said I could only stay a few minutes because you need to rest." I gave her an awkward hug. "I'll see you in the morning, huh?"

She tried to smile. "You stay out of trouble tonight."

"Sure. Not even Bonnie will tempt me tonight." She gave a little laugh that seemed to hurt her. "Good night," I said.

"Good night, Steady."

Outside I suddenly felt like baying at the moon, yelling at the top of my lungs—anything to let the pressure out. I wanted to find the nearest party and have about a dozen drinks. But, of course, I couldn't. Not after my girlfriend— the one I'd planned to dump this evening—had taken a pretty fair shot at bleeding to death. I drove home, made some popcorn, and watched TV until the network switched to the countdown for the New Year. Yippee, I thought, hell of a start.

Mom touched my shoulder. "There's a girl on the phone. She sounds upset."

I jumped up, the events of the previous day roaring through my foggy brain. "Upset? How?"

"Angry, I think."

Melissa was at the kitchen table and groaned in mock disgust. "Mom, why do you always let him traipse around in his underwear? It's disgusting."

Mom didn't give her usual reply: "Men in this family have always been a bit on the coarse side." Instead she said, "Hush, Melissa."

I picked up the phone. "Hello."

"Kinkaid? What the hell is going on?" The Tiger's voice.

"What are you talking about, Bonnie?"

"You know damn well what I'm talking about. I ran into one of the nurse's aides from the emergency room. She said you brought Sheila in yesterday afternoon with a vaginal hemorrhage."

"Ya, I did. They got the bleeding stopped and kept her overnight. Hey, what the hell are you so mad about?"

"Why didn't you call me? She's my friend too, you know."

"Well, I'm sorry, but I don't think you could have done anything."

"Maybe not, but I had a right to know."

There was a pause. We stood at opposite ends of the phone line fuming at each other. I took a deep breath.

"O.k., Bonnie. Maybe I should have, but I didn't. Now I'm going in to see her in a few minutes. I'll pick you up, if you like."

"Do that." She hung up.

Mom and Melissa were watching me. "I'll tell you about it in a minute," I said. I went back to my bedroom to get dressed.

Back in the kitchen, I said, "Mel, I really need to talk to Mom alone for a few minutes."

Melissa glared at me. "I'm a big girl now, you know."

"Ya, of course you are. But this is pretty private. Come on, Mel, give me a break, huh?" She grumbled, but went.

I told Mom everything, including the fact that whatever the nurse's suspicions, Sheila and I had not been sleeping together, and whatever was wrong had nothing to do with a torn hymen or a miscarriage or anything like that. Mom listened and seemed to believe me. "Well," she said, "I've heard about bleeding like this before. It probably seemed a lot worse than it was. She'll get good care at the hospital."

Bonnie got in the car, and we drove slowly toward the hospital. It was snowing like hell. We were almost there before she spoke. "Well, did this start during your little skiing weekend?"

I slammed on the brakes and skidded the car to the curb. I turned to face her. "How the hell do you know where we were last weekend?"

"Word gets around." She bared her teeth at me, but it was more snarl than smile. "Well, tell me, Kinkaid. Did it start when you guys got at it in whatever scumbag motel you found?"

"You've got no goddamn right to ask me that! As a matter of fact, it didn't, and for all I know, Sheila's still a virgin. Now get the hell out of my car before I break your neck."

She swung at me, fist closed. I dodged it and grabbed her

wrist. She swung with the other hand, and I had that one too. She didn't give up and tried to kick me. I slammed her back against the door. Our eyes locked in pure hatred. "You're a bastard, Kinkaid."

"And you're a bitch. Now do you want to get out of this car or do I throw you out?" I let her go—if she took another swing, so help me, I was going to nail her. She threw open the door and jumped out, leaving it open. "Stay out of my way, Tiger," I yelled at her back. She didn't turn.

I was told at the desk on the third floor that Sheila was having an ultrasound test. I walked down to the small waiting room. Mrs. Porter was already there. "Hi," I said. "I hope you didn't walk."

She smiled. "Oh, no. I called a taxi. The poker game made me rich."

"Oh, ya? Well, I'm glad to hear it."

I sat next to her and paged nervously through a magazine. She sat with her purse on her lap, smiling faintly at nothing in particular. Maybe I should try to talk to her, but what was I supposed to say? I wasn't good at dealing with weirdness. I heard Bonnie outside in the hall, talking to one of the floor nurses. I concentrated on the magazine. Bonnie came in, sat, and lit a cigarette. I didn't look up.

A nurse came in a few minutes later. "The doctor would like to see you now, Mrs. Porter." The nurse looked uncertain for a moment. "Sheila wants her boyfriend included too. If you don't—"

"No, that's fine," Mrs. Porter said.

For the life of me, I don't know why I said, "Bonnie's a friend too. I think she ought to be included." Bonnie stared at me in surprise, then made her face impassive.

The nurse said, "Well, even having you there is highly irregular."

I looked at her stubbornly. "Sheila would want her to hear."

"Well, I can ask Sheila if it's all right, but the doctor may still say no." She left.

I picked up the magazine again, uninterested in exchanging any glances with Bonnie. The nurse came back. "This way, please." At the door of the doctor's office, she explained Bonnie's presence.

The doctor—a short, middle-aged guy—nodded and waved us to chairs. He introduced himself as Dr. Belke, shuffled some papers with delicate fingers, and began. "Our physical exam revealed a growth in Sheila's lower abdomen in the vicinity of the ovaries. The ultrasound test confirmed the existence of the growth and also revealed that one of the ovaries is enlarged."

"Is she pregnant?" Mrs. Porter asked.

"No. This is a tumor, Mrs. Porter. In young women, these tumors are usually benign—not cancerous, that is. Still, there is a chance that it is malignant. We'll have to remove the tumor and test it to find out. Now Sheila is young and strong, but there can be problems with any surgery: excessive bleeding, infection, or complications from the anesthetic. I don't think you should be overly concerned about any of them." He waited for the old lady to react. She didn't. "So, if you'll sign the consent form, we'll operate tomorrow."

"Well, I suppose that would be all right. I imagine this will be very expensive."

The doctor looked surprised and shot Bonnie and me a quick glance. "Well, yes, fairly expensive, but according to the form here, you seem to have good insurance coverage."

"Oh, yes. Mr. Porter was always very careful about such things."

The doctor waited for her to say more. She didn't. "Well,

then, if you will just sign the form, I think we can proceed."
He showed her where to sign. "Do either of you young
people have any questions?"

Bonnie spoke before I did. "Have you told Sheila?"

"Yes. She took it fine. Of course, she's apprehensive, but I
assured her that the chances are good that it will be a rela-
tively simple operation with a complete recovery. If all goes
well, we'll send her home in ten days or so. You can see her
now."

In the hallway, Mrs. Porter excused herself and went into
the ladies' room. I turned on Bonnie. "Let's not apologize
or say anything about 'appreciating it' this time, huh? I
wanted you there because Sheila's going to need both of us.
The old lady has about as much sense as a cabbage, so we're
going to have to pick up the slack. Let's just plan it so we
see as little of each other as possible."

"That'll suit me fine," she snapped.

"Good. You visit her after school. I'll come in the evenings. If I'm playing ball, we'll switch."

"I volunteer Wednesday and Friday evenings. Do I have
your *permission* to see her then?"

"Just can the sarcasm, huh? If you drop in, I'll try to smile
for Sheila's sake. So are we agreed?" She nodded coldly.
Mrs. Porter came out of the rest room. I said, "You two go
in and see Sheila. I'll wait."

I went back to the visitors' lounge. Someone had left a
pack of Marlboros and some matches on the table. I took a
cigarette and lit it. I hadn't smoked one in a year, and it
made me cough. I smoked half of it anyway, then dug in my
pockets for some gum. Just like a kid, I thought, afraid
someone will smell tobacco on your breath.

They stayed with Sheila about half an hour. I offered to
give Mrs. Porter a ride home, but she said she'd call a cab. I
didn't ask Bonnie how she'd get home—a little frostbite
might do her good.

Sheila was propped up in bed and looked pretty good. "Hi, Jerr-o. 'Bout time you showed up. Close the door; we've got to plan how to bust out of this joint."

I smiled. "Not a chance, they've got the building surrounded."

"Details. Come on, give me a kiss." I did. "I figure that we can jump a couple of nurses and dress in their uniforms."

"I've seen a couple of them I wouldn't mind jumping."

She snatched the plastic water pitcher from the bedstand and threw it at me. I ducked. Shredded paper eddied around me. She laughed. "Sucker. Oldest trick in the book."

"You're nuts!" I scooped paper off the end of her bed. "They'll kill you if they see this."

She reached out, grabbed me by the nose, and pulled me close. "I wish it had been water. The only one you're ever going to jump is me, fella."

"Ouch. Let go, Sheila."

"You sound funny." She let go. I got down on my hands and knees to sweep up the paper on the floor. She addressed an unseen audience. "Can you imagine the humiliation? I'm in here less than twenty-four hours, and my steady is talking about jumping nurses. Here I lie, literally on my death bed, and . . ." She started to cry. "And it might really be," she sobbed. "I might really die."

I stumbled up and got my arms around her. "Knock it off, Sheila. Just don't talk like that."

"But, Jerr-o, the doctor said I might have cancer."

"I know, I know. But it's a real small chance. Just a tiny chance. Kids our age hardly ever get cancer. You're going to have a simple operation, and then they're going to let you out."

She snuffled. "But I'm so scared. And kids our age do get cancer. I saw a movie once—"

"That was a movie, Sheila. This is reality. Now just don't think about the chance in a hundred thousand. Come on, let me get the paper cleaned up, and we'll watch some TV."

We sat holding hands and watching television for most of the rest of the day. When she fell asleep, I walked back to the visitors' lounge. The forgotten pack of cigarettes still lay on the table, and I smoked another one. Well, this is one hell of a fix, I thought. Nothing to do but stick with her until she's well. After that? Jesus, don't think about that now, Kinkaid. For once, try not to be a selfish bastard.

In Bonnie's opinion, I really was a bastard. Cripes, she'd even tried to slug me. Why, for God's sake? We'd never liked each other, but her dislike had turned to hate. To hell with it; the girl was just crazy.

I stubbed out the cigarette and walked back to Sheila's room. She was awake, staring without interest at a football game. "Hi. Did you have a nice nap?"

"Ya. I didn't sleep very well last night."

"I can understand that."

"Jerr-o, I'm worried about Granny. I mean, I've been doing most of the stuff around the house for years now."

"She'll be o.k. People will look in on her."

"No, they won't. Even those old biddies she plays cards with never come to the house. Nobody cares about Granny, just like no one ever cared about me."

"Oh, come on, Sheila. I've never heard you talk like that before. You've just got the blues. Let's find something funny to watch."

I found a comedy rerun. After a few minutes, Sheila reached out for my hand. "I'm sorry, Steady. I didn't mean that. It's just kind of hard not to feel sorry for myself right now. I mean, they're going to cut me open, and I'll have a great big scar for the rest of my life."

"I think it'll fade pretty fast. Don't worry, I'll still try to grope your bod." I stuck a hand under the covers.

She giggled in spite of herself and fought to catch it. "Stop that. I'm a sick person."

I took my hand away. "Besides, just think about all the funny stuff you'll have to tell when you get out."

She grinned. "Ya, all about how Sheila Porter terrorized the hospital."

"The place will never be the same. They'll name a wing for you."

"Heck, I want them to rename the whole hospital for me."

When the show was over, I got up to look out the window. The world had lost definition in the storm. The blowing snow faded the outline of the dark channel winding downriver between the reaching shelves of shore ice. On the far bank, the trees were charcoal ghosts against the whiteness beyond. "Is it still snowing hard?" Sheila asked.

"Ya, it's really coming down. I'd better get home before dark."

"Are you coming back tonight?"

I hesitated. God, I didn't want to. "I'd better not chance the roads. I'll come in the morning before the operation." I went back to her bed, leaned down, and kissed her.

She held me by the shirtfront. "You could stay here. There's room for two."

"How would you explain the extra lump in the bed?"

"Details. I'd think of something." I gave her another kiss, and she let me go.

All evening I kept reminding myself that I'd told Sheila the truth: her chances of having cancer were almost nonexistent. Just stay calm, I told myself. No sense in everybody getting worked up over this thing.

SEVEN

Phil was leaning against the wall across from the door leading to the student parking lot. "Hi. Heard anything new?"
he asked.

I shook my head. "Nothing since I talked to you last
night." We headed up the hall. "Are a lot of people talking
about Sheila?"

"I heard a couple of people mention that she was in the
hospital. The news gets around quick."

"Damn. I don't want to talk to anybody about it. Not
even the doctors know what's going on yet."

"Just tell people that. When are you leaving?"

"I've got a note to get out around eleven. They're going
to operate early this afternoon. I've got to tell Burke that I'll
be missing practice."

"I'm sure that'll break your heart." He paused at a corner.
"I've got a class down this way. Wish Sheila luck for me.
She's a good kid. I'm sorry this happened."

"Me too." We stood for a moment without saying anything. I'm sure he was thinking about what I'd never had a chance to say to Sheila New Year's Eve. "Well, she'll be o.k. in a few weeks," I said. "I'll call you later."

When I got to the hospital, they'd already given Sheila a tranquilizer to calm her down before the operation. We talked some, but she kept her eyes closed a lot of the time. They came for her a little before one o'clock. "Good luck," I told her.

"Sure. Lucky, that's me."

I had some lunch in the cafeteria, then went back to the visitors' lounge and read a novel for English. It wasn't a grabber, but I forced myself to concentrate. Bonnie came in around three. I'd never seen her in anything but jeans and a sweatshirt or blouse, and she looked oddly feminine in her red-and-white-striped uniform. For a second, I was almost glad to see her. "Hi, Tiger."

"Hi, Kinkaid. What do you know?"

"Not much. They've had her down there a couple of hours."

"Where's Mrs. Porter?"

"At the senior citizens' center, I think. She came to see Sheila this morning before I got here."

"Strange she didn't stay."

"Well, you hit the nail on the head; she's strange."

"One of these days we should have a long talk about your love of clichés."

"Tiger, don't start on me, huh?"

"Sorry, force of habit." She sat and lit a cigarette. "Want one?"

I looked at her sharply. "No."

"You don't have to bite my head off; I was just being polite."

"That must be difficult for you."

"To you, yes. Very difficult."

The novel was in my right hand, and I felt the pages squeezing off the circulation in the forefinger I'd inserted to keep my place. I opened the book and stuck in a scrap of paper. Well, who'd had the better of it this time? "I thought we were going to call a truce for a few days."

"I guess we were, but it's tough. You bring out the worst in me."

I could have given her a good shot on that one, but her tone was different this time—almost like she'd been talking to herself. She wasn't looking at me, but at the square of blue sky visible in the high window. Pensive. Ya, that was the word you used when a person sat staring into space while gnawing a fingernail. I opened the novel again and read a paragraph.

Bonnie crushed her cigarette in the ashtray and glanced at her watch. "They should be done by now. A nurse told me yesterday that the operation usually takes about an hour with an hour or so in the recovery room afterward. I'm going down to see what I can find out." I nodded, but didn't look up.

Bonnie helped wheel Sheila down the hall, then stood back while two nurses got Sheila into bed. I watched through the open door. Something had gone wrong; I could feel it in the way the nurses talked to Sheila. Paranoia, I told myself. Hell, the girl just got cut open; no wonder they're handling her so carefully. Sheila was limp, her eyes closed. When one of the nurses spoke to her, she only nodded slightly.

Bonnie came into the hall and pulled me a few steps away. Dark hair and the smell of her brushed my cheek when I leaned down to listen. "I'm going back downstairs to eavesdrop. They wouldn't tell me anything outright."

101

"Do you think there's something wrong?"

"I'm not sure. Something's odd. I saw the doctor, and he didn't look happy."

"Maybe we ought to call her grandmother."

"We'll worry about her later. Just stay with Sheila now."

I went into the room after the nurses left. I took Sheila's hand. "Hi."

She smiled, but didn't open her eyes. "Hi, Steady." A moment later she was asleep. I waited. A nurse came in and checked Sheila's blood pressure. I was considering going down to the lounge when Bonnie came to the door and beckoned. She looked grim. I eased my fingers out of Sheila's and went into the hall.

"I couldn't find out much for sure, but people are pretty down. I heard one nurse say that the tumor was the size of a football."

"A football? My God, how could it fit?"

"I've heard of tumors that big before. I guess there's just a lot more space than you'd think. The nurse also said it had a 'beefy red' color."

"What does that mean?"

"Hell, I don't know, but the other nurse shook her head like it wasn't a good sign. Everyone's pissed that old lady Porter isn't around. They sent someone to get her."

Dr. Belke looked tired, his smile of greeting forced when we followed Mrs. Porter into his office. "Sheila handled the operation fine. We removed the tumor and sent it to the lab for testing." He paused. "We found some troubling signs, however. The tumor did not have a normal color, and there were indications it had been there for some time. We were also disturbed to find what appeared to be some seeding on the lining of the abdomen and the layer of fat that hangs in front of the bowel." He took paper and pen, sketched a torso, and pointed out the areas.

"What do you mean by seeding?" I asked.

"Multiple small tumors. We see them as shiny white spots."

"Is it cancer?" Bonnie asked quietly.

"We can't be sure until the pathologist's report on the tumor is complete. That'll take a couple of days." He looked closely at Mrs. Porter, whose attention seemed fixed on the sketch. "However, I think cancer is a very definite possibility."

Bonnie said very softly, "Oh, shit."

I felt like somebody Gary's size had grabbed me around the chest from behind and was squeezing as hard as he could. I got my breath. "But you could do something about that, couldn't you? I mean with radiation and drugs and stuff."

"In many cases, not all. But let's not worry about that right now. First we need the pathologist's report. Until we have it, I'd recommend that we do not tell Sheila our worries. She'll be tired and sore, and she won't be able to eat or drink anything. Those are enough problems for the next couple of days."

Out in the hall, Mrs. Porter didn't say a word. She walked slowly to the elevator, pushed the down button, and waited. The door opened, then closed behind her. After a long moment, Bonnie said, "Come on, let's get a Coke and think about this a little bit. Sheila will sleep for a while yet."

We drank Cokes in the cafeteria. There wasn't much to say or even to think about. We'd just have to wait it out until they knew one way or the other. We went back to Sheila's room wearing the most optimistic expressions we could muster.

Sheila was still asleep. Bonnie fidgeted for a few minutes, then excused herself to do her volunteer work. I tried to read. Now and then Sheila would wake up for a minute or two. Once when a nurse came in to take her blood pressure,

Sheila snapped, "You just did that." The nurse smiled, took the reading, and left. "Jeez, why can't they let me have some sleep? I mean, every five minutes—"

"It was more like forty-five minutes," I said.

"Bull." She started coughing. She held her hands to her stomach and tried to stop. "Oh, Christ, Jerr-o, it hurts. Get me a glass of water."

"I can't. They said your stomach's got to be empty for a while."

She curled on her side and got the coughing stopped. Her face was shiny with perspiration. "God, my throat's sore." She stifled another cough.

"They had a tube down your throat during the operation to help you breathe. The pain is supposed to go away soon."

She groaned again. "Oh, God, Jerr-o. This is torture."

I felt a lump in my own throat. "I'll go see if it's time for your shot. Just hold on."

The nurse at the desk checked her schedule, then went into the room. She lifted the sheet, and I had a glimpse of Sheila's bare backside. I turned away. Bonnie was standing a couple of feet behind me, a tray of food in her hands. What did her eyes say? "What's the matter, Kinkaid? Can't take it?" Or was it "What's the matter? Can't stand to see your girl's ass anymore?" She held out the food. "Here. Sheila can't eat it. You might as well."

"I couldn't," I said.

"Yes, you can. Take it down to the lounge. I can be with Sheila for a few minutes now."

I was hungrier than I'd imagined and thankful that Bonnie had thought to bring me the tray. When I got back to the room, I said, "Thanks. I left the tray on a food cart."

Bonnie got up. "You're welcome. I'm going home for a while. I'll bring back some homework and do it here."

"Where do you think Mrs. Porter is?"

She shrugged. "Let somebody else worry about her. Sheila isn't noticing much right now." I nodded and settled back with the novel.

Mrs. Porter finally showed up around seven-thirty. She sat down without a word and stared at Sheila. "Hi," I said. "She's been asleep most of the afternoon." She didn't seem to hear me. I spoke a little louder. "She's in some pain, but they're giving her morphine. If she asks for water or anything, we're supposed to say no." She didn't reply. "Anyway, if you're going to be here for a while, I've really got to go . . ." I'd meant to say "go home," but a whiff of the air she'd brought with her stopped me. My God, the old lady reeked of booze. "Ah, I've really got to go to the bathroom," I finished lamely.

"Why do they have her connected to that bottle?" Her words were slurred.

"For fluids. Ah, as I said, she can't have anything to drink or eat. Not for about four days."

"She's got to eat. She's just a slip of a girl."

A slip of a girl? No one had ever accused Sheila of that. At least not in a long time. "Well, I guess they're worried about her throwing up. They told us that's standard procedure after abdominal operations. Not allowing them to eat or drink, that is." Cripes, I was sounding as fuzzy as the old lady. She continued staring at Sheila. "I'll be back in a minute," I said.

I used the rest room next to the visitors' lounge. What the hell should I do about the old lady? Nothing. Cripes, not all of this was my problem. I washed my hands and face and came out. A nurse was waiting for me. "Young man, that woman in Sheila Porter's room is intoxicated!"

"Ya, I know."

"Well, somebody has to get her out of here. She just vomited all over herself."

Oh, shit. The nurse stood there staring at me as if I'd

gotten the old lady drunk. "Hey, ah, you know, I'm just . . ." Damn. "Look, can you get her cleaned up? I'll call somebody."

One of the nurses—a friendlier one this time—helped me get Mrs. Porter down to the main floor and out to my car. We had to stop in the middle of the parking lot to let her heave again. In the car, Mrs. Porter slumped against the door, breathing heavily through her mouth. She rode all the way to Bonnie's that way.

Bonnie hopped in the backseat without a word, and we drove to Sheila's. It took one of us on either side to get Mrs. Porter into the house. An empty bottle of Rhine wine and half a dozen beer cans stood on the kitchen counter. While Bonnie got her in bed, I went to the bathroom to wash the puke smell off my hands. The towels Sheila had soaked with blood two days before still lay in the corner where I'd kicked them. Oh, my God, I thought.

I went back to the living room and surveyed the small room. Bonnie came out of the bedroom. "God, is this place a mess," she said.

"Check out the corner of the bathroom."

She looked a little shaken when she came back. For the first time since I'd known her, something had gotten to the Tiger. She sat down and lit a cigarette. I took a cigarette from her pack and held it up. "Can we keep this between you and me?" She nodded, and I lit it. "How the hell did she do it in two days?" I asked. "I mean, this place was never very clean or orderly, but, cripes . . ."

Bonnie took a deep breath. "Well, we can't leave it like this. Why don't you do the kitchen, and I'll do my best with the rest?" I nodded. She half rose, then sat down again. "Screw it, let's sit for another minute."

"What are we going to do about Mrs. Porter? I mean, she

106

can't come to the hospital drunk. And she can't let things go to hell like this." I gestured around the room. "Even if Sheila doesn't have cancer, she won't be able to do much of the work for a while."

"Sheila's got cancer. I'm almost positive of that. The doctor was just blowing a little smoke, giving us a chance to adjust to the idea before confirming it."

"Now wait a second, how can you be so sure?"

"I'm not completely, and I imagine he's holding open the chance that it isn't cancer." She took a deep breath. "But after I left you the last time, I got one of the nurses down on the first floor to talk about that seeding business. It's a very bad sign. And the color of the tumor too. I was going to call and tell you later. Or maybe I wasn't. I don't know."

I sat staring at my hands and the slow wisp of smoke drifting up from my cigarette. My God, this couldn't be happening to Sheila. It couldn't be happening to me. Bonnie said quietly, "Maybe we shouldn't think too much right now. Maybe I'm wrong. Let's get this place cleaned up."

I was halfway through the dishes when Bonnie came into the kitchen. "I can't find anything to clean the bathroom floor. I'll have to go home for something." I handed her my car keys. "Sure you trust me?" she asked.

"I don't think trust was ever the problem."

"From you, I'll take that as a compliment. Back in a few minutes."

I finished the dishes and made the mistake of glancing in the refrigerator. Some of the stuff had been there a very long time. Oh, Sheila, I thought. How bad were you really feeling? I started pulling out moldy leftovers. I didn't even have to get my nose close to the half-gallon of milk to know it was sour. I heard a car door slam outside, and Bonnie came into the house with an armload of cleaning supplies.

She stared at the leftovers. "God," she said, "there must be a fortune in penicillin growing in this mold." I grunted. "Have you looked in on the old lady recently?" she asked.

"Ya, she's in the pink of condition."

"That's an old one. But classy. Where do you get all those, anyway?"

I turned on her. "You know, if you weren't always saying dumb stuff like that, we might actually get along for more than ten minutes at a stretch."

"That would be a problem, wouldn't it? For the record, I did like your comment that Mrs. Porter didn't have the sense of a cabbage. That was an improvement."

"And 'for the record' is a cliché."

She laughed. "Not bad. There's hope for your mental development yet. Come on, forget it. You said it yesterday, I'm a bitch." She went to the sink and started running more dishwater.

Around eleven o'clock, we stood in the middle of the kitchen and surveyed our work. The place wasn't exactly ready for a Marine inspection, but we'd reorganized the clutter and scraped off the top layer of dust, dirt, and grime. Bonnie brushed a stray lock of hair from her damp forehead. Her blouse was stained with dark rings of sweat under the arms, and I could feel my shirt clinging to my back. "God," she said, "it must be ninety in here. Is there any beer in the fridge?"

"Ya, quite a bit of it."

"The old lady will never miss a couple of cans. I think we've earned it."

She got out two and handed one to me. I offered a toast. "As Phil would say, 'Screw training.'"

She laughed and passed me the cigarettes. "You know, I wouldn't get so mad at you jocks about the letters thing if you weren't so damn hypocritical about the training stuff."

I shrugged. "We don't make the rules; we just break them every once in a while. Then we take our chances and don't cry if we get caught."

"Ya, but why do you say training rules are a reason for not giving letters in nonathletic activities? I mean, hell, we all know most of you drink and smoke sometimes."

"I don't know if it's most. I don't think Gary ever does—Crap. Do we really have to talk about this now?"

She sighed. "No, I was stupid to bring it up. I just go into automatic sometimes." She stared at the floor, absently turning the beer can in her fingers, then leaned down to scrape a small wad of something off the linoleum with a fingernail. I got a quick shot of cleavage. Nice. She straightened, and I glanced away. "I've been thinking more about Sheila's grandmother," she said. "I'm not sure we should have done all this cleaning. Maybe we should have called someone. If a social worker had seen the mess, maybe the old lady would have been put in a nursing home or something."

"Sheila's got to have a place to come home to."

"Ya, that's true. Well, maybe the old lady will straighten up."

I finished my beer and dropped the can in the trash. "Ready?"

"Let me look in on the old lady again." She was back in a minute. "She's snoring. Boy, is she going to have a hangover." She handed me a plastic bag. "Can you handle doing the towels?"

"Ya, I can handle it."

"Thought you could. I'd do them, but Dad's got the washing machine spread all over the basement. It'll be a week before he gets around to putting it back together."

"Why don't you fix it? Sounds to me like something *you* could handle."

She pulled on her coat. "Male egos, Kinkaid. You've got to be careful with them."

"Surprises me that the concept had ever occurred to you."

She gave me a look of at least feigned respect. "You know, I think there definitely is hope for you. Just don't let it go to your head."

"That's another cliché."

"Careful. You're doing just what I warned you about. Let's go. I'm bushed, and I need a shower."

For a crazy second, I almost said, "Want company?"

EIGHT

Mom held up one of the towels and studied it critically. "I'm not sure these are going to come clean. I'd just throw them away."

I rubbed my eyes. It was nearly midnight, and I was exhausted. "I don't think we can do that, Mom. They don't have much."

"Well, maybe some extra bleach will help." She dumped the towels into the washer and poured bleach. "This was worse than I thought; she bled a lot."

"It was pretty bad. . . . Things are getting worse too." I tried to summarize the events of the day, but suddenly everything seemed too confused to explain. I put my head in my hands for a moment. "I don't know, Mom. It's just a hell of a deal."

"You need some sleep, dear." She glanced at her watch. "And I've got to get to work, or the three of us will end up on the breadline. You can tell me more about Sheila tomorrow." She started for the stairs, then paused to put a hand on my shoulder. "Things will seem brighter in the morning, dear. Come on; up to bed with you."

"I've got to do some homework."

"No, you don't. Tomorrow's Friday. You can catch up over the weekend."

"Ya, I guess. . . . I need a note for tomorrow. I'm going to stop by the hospital on my way to school, and I might not make homeroom."

"I'll leave one on the table. Make sure Melissa knows she has to be ready in time to ride the bus."

Sheila slumped down in the bed when I came into her room. "Water. Give me water, Gunga Dee. Water, beer, gin, whiskey, even Dr Pepper." She let her head fall to the side and lay with her tongue protruding. I applauded. She opened her eyes and grinned. "I've still got it, huh?"

"You're better than ever." I kissed her and sat on the chair by the bed. "I think it's Gunga Din, though."

"Details." She pulled herself up a little. "Ouch." She compressed her lips and struggled until she got herself comfortable. "What did they do to this beautiful body?" She lifted the covers to look. "My God, I'm ruined!"

"You'll be o.k. soon," I said and realized that could well be a lie.

She dropped the covers and stared at me hard. "What have they told you?"

I lied. "Not much. The doctor said they have to wait for the lab report."

"Ya, he said that to me too. The bathologist's report."

"Pathologist's."

"Stop correcting me!"

"Sorry."

She sighed and reached for my hand. "I'm sorry, Steady. I didn't mean to snap at you." She spent a moment staring at the ceiling. "Details. God, how I hate details. That's why I

always do so lousy in history. Who said what? When did so-
and-so do this? Where is this city, where's that city? Bullshit. Details. Same difference." I didn't say anything. "And
now I've got to wait for some dope to make a *detailed* report
before I can find out if I'm going to die or not." She bit her
lip.

"Don't talk that way. Think about something else."

"Like what?" she said bitterly. "Bonnie said the same
thing this morning. Cripes, you even sound like her."

I jerked my hand away. "Now that's an insult! Just because you're in the hospital, Sheila Porter, don't think you
can start hurling insults at your steady." I got up and started
to pace angrily.

Sheila gave me a confused look, then caught on and
started to giggle. "Stop it. Don't make me laugh." She put
her hands over her abdomen. "Stop, it hurts." I sat and she
took my hand. "God, you're a lousy actor, Jerr-o. But I love
you anyway."

"Thanks."

"Do you love me?"

"Sure."

"Say, 'I love you.'" I did. She smiled and closed her eyes.
"It feels good to hear you say it. Keep saying it, and I'll get
well. And when I get out, watch out world. Porter and
Kinkaid are going to be hot." She looked at me. "Right,
Jerr-o?"

"Right. . . . Hey, look, Sheila, I've got to get to school
soon."

"Just like Bonnie again. Come for a few minutes then
leave me to the mercy of sawbones and all these other people in white clothes. Jesus, all the damn white around here.
No imagination."

"I'll come back this evening after the game."

She looked hurt. "You've got to play basketball?"

"You know I do."

"It's a home game, isn't it? Can't you come up after school?"

"I just can't, Sheila. Burke scheduled extra practice. He said we're going to learn to shoot free throws if we have to practice right up to game time. . . . Look, I'm sure Bonnie will be up to see you, and I'll stay as long as you want me to after the game. O.k.?"

"I'm going to miss you, Steady."

"I'll miss you too. Listen to the game on the radio. I'll be a star for you."

She smiled. "I know you will."

The ref blew his whistle and pointed to Phil. Phil raised his hand. Third foul and it wasn't halftime yet. I wanted in. Needed to be in. Burke didn't look at me, but gestured to Hastreiter sitting to my right. Shit. Miss one practice, and I was no longer first replacement.

Phil sat down beside me. "No way did I foul that kid. The ref blew the call." He wiped sweat from his face with a towel, eyes intent on the game. "That's it! Way to go, Mike." Mike sprinted downcourt with a steal and laid it in. We clapped. "If Gary can keep beating their center, we'll have this one." He glanced at me. "Come on, say something. Burke will put you in next quarter."

I shrugged. Gary intercepted a pass and threw a nice outlet to Hastreiter, who let go a long one just as time ran out in the half. Bingo. "Not if Haz keeps shooting like that."

"Luck. Come on, let's go." We trooped to the locker room. We were up by 3, and Burke gave us the usual song and dance about bearing down and playing with pride.

Mike was sitting next to me. "How's Sheila doing?" he whispered.

"O.k. so far. We're waiting for the report on the tumor."

"Well, let me know if I can help. There are a couple of old dudes up on the rez who do some bizarre stuff with mushrooms. Old Indian medicine—may not cure you, but you don't much give a shit after you take it." I hid a grin by rubbing a cheek.

"All right, men," Burke said. "Let's go out and get 'em."

Get 'em. Right. Three minutes into the second half, Gary was out with a twisted ankle and Phil had his fourth foul. Phil growled something as he left the court, and the ref came over and said, "I could have called a technical on that one, Coach. Keep your boys cool." Burke nodded and glared at Phil, who was sitting with a towel over his head.

Hastreiter went in, and I waited. Phil took the towel off his head and watched the game morosely. "Damn. We could have had them."

A couple of minutes later, Burke pulled Mike for a breather, and I went in. They were inching ahead, and we were weak inside with Gary out. Haz and I started shooting long. Neither of us had much of a touch. Down by 8, Burke called time, then put in Mike, Phil, and a limping Gary.

On the bench, I felt someone lean down beside me. I turned. Bev Knutson was there, looking worried. "Bonnie said to get to the hospital right after the game."

"Why? What happened?"

"She didn't say, but she sounded upset and in a hurry."

"Keep your mind in the game, Kinkaid," Burke called. "You can talk to the girls afterward."

"Thanks, Bev. I'll get out of here as fast as I can."

I waited, watching the seconds on the game clock tick down. What now? Was Mrs. Porter drunk again? Or had something happened to Sheila? A whistle blew, and Phil headed for the sidelines, his face grim. Burke yelled, "Kinkaid, get in there. We can beat 'em yet." That was a joke; we were already out of it. In the locker room, Burke

115

spent ten minutes giving us hell for letting another one slip away.

Bonnie was waiting for me when I got out of the elevator on the third floor. "Come into the lounge." I followed her. She sat, lit a cigarette, and tossed the pack to me. She studied the floor, then spoke, trying to keep her voice even. "It's cancer. They got the pathologist's report back early, and it's bad, very bad. The cancer is all over her insides— the liver, diaphragm, all sorts of stuff." She had to pause for a second. "The doctor told Sheila and her grandmother about an hour ago. He called the situation 'very grave.'"

I slumped. It couldn't be. Not really. A long minute passed before I could trust my voice. "What does 'very grave' mean?"

She took a deep breath. "It means she's probably going to die. This is a rare form of cancer without any treatment. Radiation doesn't work on it, and there aren't any proven drugs. The doctor said they can try one new drug, but the cancer's probably gone too far for it to do much good."

For maybe three minutes, we sat in silence, the hushed sounds of the hospital coming distantly to us. We were both playing the game of keeping control at any cost, and we didn't risk looking at each other. Finally, I asked, "How did Sheila take it?"

"I wasn't even there. They sent me downstairs with some records, and the doctor came while I was gone. I don't know, maybe they were trying to get me out of the way. I was coming back when I heard Sheila sobbing. A nurse was in with her, giving her a shot. Dr. Belke was in the hall explaining everything to the old lady. I listened, then went in and held Sheila's hand until she fell asleep." Suddenly, Bonnie slammed a fist against the chair arm. "I mean I just sat, Kinkaid! Just sat without one damn thing to say!" She stared at me with blazing eyes, then turned quickly away.

"I'm not sure there was a hell of a lot you could say, Tiger. . . . What did the old lady do?"

"Her? Hell, she just sat in a corner as far away as she could get. She's still there as far as I know. After Sheila fell asleep, I came out and called Bev. Then when I figured the game was over, I went to the elevator to wait for you."

"Thanks." My brain was trying to get some kind of handle on things and not doing worth a damn. I got up and stared through the window at the cold night. Calm down, I told myself. Don't lose it now.

Neither of us spoke for a while. Finally, Bonnie said, "If you're up to it, maybe we ought to go in and see her." I nodded.

Mrs. Porter looked up from her corner when we came into Sheila's room. She rose and walked out without speaking. I thought Sheila was asleep, but when I leaned down to kiss her on the cheek, she grabbed me with both arms and pulled me down hard. The motion must have hurt her bad, because she let out a sob of pain. Then she was whispering fiercely in my ear, "I'm not going to die, Jerr-o! They can't make me, and I won't. I just won't do it!"

I held her gently. "Hey, it's o.k. Take it easy."

"I won't do it, Jerr-o!"

"No, of course not."

A nurse came in quickly. "Oh, you can't do that! She's much too sick." She took one of Sheila's wrists firmly. "Now, come on. Let go. You're going to tear out those stitches." She got us separated. "There. Now be a good girl, Sheila. The doctor said you're supposed to be quiet and get some rest." She checked Sheila's pulse and blood pressure. "Now in half an hour, we'll have something more to help you get to sleep."

"I don't want to go to sleep. And you gave me something just a little while ago."

"That was *quite* a while ago. Now, just stay calm. You can

117

talk or watch TV, but no more hugging." She glanced at Bonnie. "We have some more errands for you, Bonnie."

I'd forgotten Bonnie was there. She stood in the corner, looking stricken. "I'll be there in a minute." She hesitated, then came to the bed. "I've got to go for a little while, Sheila. I'll come back for a few minutes before I go home." Bonnie looked at me for a second, and I swore the Tiger's eyes were moist.

Sheila said, "Turn on the TV, Jerr-o. I've had it with all this crap; I want to watch somebody act."

After a while, her hand twitched under mine, and she fell asleep. The nurse came in, turned off the TV, and beckoned me into the hall. "She'll probably sleep now. We'll give her another sedative if she wakes up. You might as well go home. We don't want to excite her more than we have to."

I headed for the elevators, relief flooding over me. I needed fresh air desperately, needed the cold to jar my brain back to life.

Bonnie was standing by the reception desk on the first floor. "Is she asleep?"

"Ya. The nurse told me to beat it."

"I think I'll go too. I've been here for six hours, and I'm not doing too well anymore."

"Sure, I'll see you tomorrow."

"Maybe I'll wait until the afternoon. . . . I think we ought to go back to our plan, you know, of dividing things up. . . . It's just too hard when we're all together." She walked away quickly, leaving me wondering why she'd put it that way.

I had to find some noise, some people. Sheila had cancer, was probably going to die, and I couldn't be alone with that knowledge yet. I glanced in at the bowling alley, but saw no one I knew well. I drove the fifteen miles to the Purple

Horse. Phil's beater Ford was in the lot. Jim Felser was just heading in, and I asked him to send Phil out. Five minutes later, Phil came through the door. "How you doing, Jerr?"

"Not so hot, Phil." I told him the news.

"Oh, shit," he muttered. "It's really that bad, huh?" I nodded. "What are you going to do?"

"What can I do but stick it out with her?"

We stood in the cold night with nothing to say. Finally, Phil said, "Well, it ain't going to do her any good if you catch pneumonia. Come on inside."

"I don't know if that'd be right, Phil."

"I think it's just what you need. Come on, it won't hurt nothing."

Lisa, Gary, Mike, Haz, and half a dozen other kids were sitting at a couple of tables in the far corner. The talk quieted as we came close. "It's o.k., guys," Phil said. "He's harmless. Just another derelict stumbling in to get warm."

Conversation resumed. We sat. Mike, Gary, and Haz moved in closer—the team gathering round, no outsiders invited. Phil leaned his chair back and gazed through the smoke at the ceiling. Well, he already knew. "How bad is it?" Gary asked.

"Real bad. Like she might not . . ." I took a deep breath. "Might not make it."

"Damn," Gary muttered.

Mike asked, "What can they do for her?"

"Not much. There's one experimental drug, but they're not very optimistic." A bottle got passed to our table. Gary started to pass it to the next, but I intercepted it, spiked my Coke, and stuck my dollar bill under the rubber band.

Phil looked around quickly. "That's dangerous, man. Not all these people are our friends."

"Since when did you go straight?" I asked. I lifted my cup. "Screw training." There was a long pause as they

119

watched me. "Look, guys, I don't want to spoil your evening. I shouldn't even be here. I just, you know, needed some noise. Go dance or something. I'm o.k. . . . Don't tell anyone what I said."

They nodded. Phil said, "Hey, Lisa, let's dance." He slapped my shoulder as he squeezed by to join Lisa. Someone asked Haz and Gary a question about the game, and they turned away to answer. I stared into my drink.

Mike's voice was quiet. "You ever need to talk, I'll be around."

"Thanks, Mike, but there isn't much to say." He nodded.

I drank a couple more, and the sides of the road were a little hazy when I drove home. Mom was already at work, and I hoped Melissa would be asleep, but I heard the sound of the TV when I opened the back door. "Hi, what's on?" I asked.

"Some old John Wayne movie. It's dumb." She stared at me appraisingly. "You've been drinking."

"Very perceptive of you." I slumped into a chair.

"One of these days you're going to get caught drinking or smoking, and Burke will kick you off the team."

"Let me worry about that."

There was a pause. "So, how's Sheila?"

What should I tell her? Cripes, she'd have the news all over school on Monday, but it probably would be anyway. "Sheila's got cancer, and it's very bad, Mel. Like maybe no cure."

Melissa was the first one to cry that night. The first one since Sheila. She went to the kitchen for tissues. I felt like kicking myself. Real good, Kinkaid. Hit her right between the eyes with it. When she came back, I said, "I'm sorry, Mel. I should have put that better."

She sat, wiped her eyes, and honked a bit. "That's o.k. Go on, tell me the details." I did. She listened red-eyed, but

120

didn't cry any more. That was Melissa, vent the emotions quick and get back to business. "So, how's Bonnie handling it?"

"Good. Bonnie's real tough."

"I'll bet she's enjoying it—getting lots of practical experience being a nurse."

I raised my eyebrows. "I don't think she's enjoying it. Since when do you dislike Bonnie? A couple of weeks ago you were telling me how neat she was."

"Since yesterday when she almost took my head off in a volleyball game."

"Come again."

"We were playing volleyball in gym with a bunch of junior girls. Nobody playing real serious, you know. Just having fun. Bonnie was on the other side of the net from me. She got set up for a spike and really smashed it. If I hadn't ducked, it would have gone right down my throat."

"Doesn't sound much like Bonnie. I didn't think she put out much when it came to sports."

"Well, she sure did that time. Then she laughed at me and said, 'Well, at least one Kinkaid has brains enough to get out of the way.' What did she mean by that?"

I shrugged. "Beats me. Bonnie just says crap sometimes. I don't think she means a lot of it."

"She meant something that time. She glared at me like she'd just as soon kill me as look at me. What's with her, anyway?"

Why the hell should I defend the Tiger? A couple of days back, she'd tried to punch me. "Hell, I don't know. She's just strange. . . . Look, I'm just beat, Mel. I've got to get some sleep."

I was at the door when she spoke. "I'm sorry about Sheila, Jerry. Real sorry."

I nodded. "Thanks."

"Sheila's on the phone!" Melissa yelled.

I dragged myself up from sleep and ran to the kitchen. Melissa snapped the elastic on the back of my underwear, and I slapped at her hand. Both were reflex actions. "Hello."

"Morning, Jerr-o. 'Bout time you got your butt out of bed. When are you coming to see me?"

"Ah, let's see. About an hour, maybe."

"Good. Stop on the way and pick up a case of 7-Up and a king-sized pizza with everything on it. Double cheese, double marshmallows. Just tell the nurse it's your breakfast."

"God, that's a terrible image for someone who hasn't eaten breakfast."

"You should complain. They haven't let me eat in three days. Come on, hop to it, Steady. We've got things to do."

"Well, you certainly seem back in form."

"Better than ever. What I really want you to do is drop by my house and pick up my algebra and any other school books you can find."

"Algebra?"

"Ya, remember that stuff with all the x's and y's? You know, all that detail stuff that math teachers think means something."

"Ya, right. I remember."

"And, Jerr-o"—her voice got serious—"check on Granny, huh? I haven't seen her or heard from her."

"Well, it's early. She'll probably come by soon."

"Just check on her, o.k.?"

"Sure."

A nurse had Sheila by the arm and was walking her slowly up the hall. The IV bottle swung from the wheeled stand Sheila was pushing with her right hand. She looked pale but determined. "Hi, Jerr-o. They say I'll be ready for the hundred-yard dash in a few days." The nurse turned her around, and they made their way slowly to the room. When she was propped up in bed again, she held out her arms for me. "Give me a hug, Steady. Sheila's on the mend. Did you bring the algebra?"

"Ya, here."

She started paging through the book. "How was Granny?"

"I didn't see her. She must have gone out early." I didn't mention that the house was a mess again with another empty wine bottle on the kitchen counter and beer cans littering the living room.

"She probably went to the senior citizens' center. I'm glad. I need some peace to work." She paged further back in the book and grimaced. "Ugh. Well, I guess I'd better start at the beginning. They say I need to pass this stupid class to graduate. And I need a diploma to get into acting school. So here goes. Sit beside me, Steady."

She worked the rest of the morning. She didn't need a lot of help with the easy stuff from the early part of the book, so I spent most of my time fidgeting. When Dr. Belke saw her doing algebra, I thought his smile had an odd twist, but Sheila didn't notice. I left the room and sat in the visitors' lounge while he was examining her. When I came back in, she hardly looked up from the algebra text. "Jerr-o, explain this stupid graph to me."

When I figured Bonnie would be in soon, I said, "I've got to go home for a while; Mel and I've got chores to do."

Sheila turned over a sheet of paper and started jotting a problem. "O.k. Say hi to Melissa for me."

"Sure. I'll see you this evening."

"O.k. I'll have a lot for you to correct."

———

She was like that for the next week. I got her assignments from school, and she spent most of her waking hours fighting through them. After the doctor let her start eating and drinking Sunday evening, I heard more complaints about the small servings than the algebra.

The news of Sheila's cancer spread around school fast, and a lot of people asked me about her. I kept it simple: "She's pretty sick, but they're doing the best they can."

It was harder when Mr. Armstrong called me down to his office. I told him the details. He shook his head. "I had the feeling something was wrong, but I thought it was probably troubles at home or something. I should have asked some questions."

"I don't think it would have made a lot of difference, Mr. Armstrong. The doctor said the cancer had been growing for quite a while."

He sighed, then managed a smile. "Well, give her my best. Tell her to get well. We'll need her for the next play. And tell her to stay away from ladders."

I smiled. "I'll do that, Mr. Armstrong."

Bonnie, Mrs. Porter, and I did our best to keep Sheila company. The old lady spent an hour or so every morning watching quiz programs with Sheila, then disappeared for the rest of the day. Bonnie came after school when I had practice and usually left before I arrived. I spent my evenings doing homework with Sheila. That was a drag, but semester finals were coming up, and I was getting a lot of work done. So everything was going smoothly. Everything, except the fact that Sheila was living in a dream, and sooner or later she'd have to wake up.

NINE

Burke had given up trying to teach us how to shoot free throws, so there was no practice before the game. Phil and I picked up a couple of Sheila's assignments, then pushed out the door into a hard west wind. "Cripes," Phil growled. "How cold is it?"

"I heard fifteen below."

"This wind makes it feel like fifty below."

We got in my car. The engine turned over with agonized slowness. "Come on, baby," I muttered. The engine caught.

"Close," Phil said.

"Too damned close. I'm going to get someone to start it up at halftime." We drove with the defroster blasting and the windows open a crack to pull our cold breath away from the windshield. "So, Sheila's home now," I said. "Do you want to go over and see her for a few minutes?"

"How's she doing?" Phil asked.

"Better than I expected. She watches TV, does her schoolwork, tries a little housework now and then. And she

125

counts off the hours until she can get that cancer drug. I mean, she's not on top of the world, but what can you expect? Why don't you come over for a few minutes? She'd really enjoy that."

He shifted uncomfortably. "I would, man, but I promised my old lady I'd get in some wood for the furnace."

I was pretty sure that was a lie, but I let it go. He'd come soon.

Sheila stared out the kitchen window at the coming dark. "I wish I could go to the game."

"It's awfully cold, Sheila. I don't think you should."

"If I don't get out of here soon, I'll go absolutely boppers."

"Bonkers."

"Details. Boppers sounds better. I bet you it wouldn't hurt me to go."

"You've only been home a couple of days. Give it a little time. . . . Did you get a lot done today?" I reached out for the papers under her algebra text.

She laid a forearm across the book. "Not enough. I had to do some cleaning."

The house didn't look like she'd done much. "I hope you took it easy." She didn't reply, but continued to stare out the window. "So, is Bonnie coming over?"

"Ya, maybe I can convince *her* to take me to the game."

Crap. She hadn't been so down since the day she'd heard the pathologist's report. "Well, let me help you get some supper started." I got up. "Will your grandmother be home for supper?"

"No, she's at a card party, as usual. . . . Jerr-o, don't worry about supper. I'll get something when I'm hungry. Just sit and talk to me for a few minutes."

I hesitated, then went back to the table. "O.k., but make something good and filling, huh?"

126

"Don't worry. My other keeper will be here before long. She'll force-feed me." I winced. After a few seconds, she reached for my hand. "I'm sorry, Steady. I'm being a bitch tonight. I just can't stand being cooped up. Tell Sheila something funny to take her mind off her troubles."

I told her the school gossip. None of it was very funny or interesting, but she didn't seem to be listening anyway. "So, that's about what I know. Finals were over today. My trig test was a pain, but the others weren't too bad. . . . Did you watch 'As the World Churns' this afternoon?"

"'As the World Turns.'"

"Details."

For the first time she looked me square in the face. Then she laughed. "Touché, or whatever they say. I walked into that one, didn't I? I think you've been practicing."

"Hard not to pick up something around here."

She smiled and squeezed my hand. "Poor Jerr-o. I really put you through it sometimes, don't I?"

"Sometimes. Come on, tell me the soap news. I'm getting addicted."

"Well, let's see." Her blues seemed to disappear as she got into describing the bizarre course of the soap's plot. "And Mora finally got her fashion show. I paid attention to her legs and thought: Hey, my legs are just as good as hers." Sheila pulled up her housecoat almost to the waist. "See. I lost weight in the hospital. No one's going to call me 'fat legs Porter' anymore. Pretty nice, huh?"

"Ah, ya. I never thought you had fat legs, though."

She let the hem drop. "Shows how much you noticed. I've lost weight some other places too. All told, eight or ten pounds. I'm going to be one of those lean, svelte types from now on."

I almost said something about having liked her just fine before, but decided against it. She didn't give me much of a chance anyway. She started describing how she thought a

127

little modeling would advance her acting career. "Heck, I'd look just as good in a pair of designer jeans as . . . what's-her-name. You know, that actress who never plucks her eyebrows. Brooke Fields or something."

"Brooke Shields."

"Ya, right. Keep those details coming. Anyway, I figure it this way, I can model anything except maybe a two-piece bathing suit because of this damn scar on my belly. But there's probably some makeup I can put on that." She hardly paused for breath in the ten minutes before Bonnie's car rolled up. "Ooops, better slip out the back way, Jerr-o. I can't stand the sight of all the blood when you two start clawing at each other." The Tiger got out of the car and opened the trunk.

"Oh, we're getting along o.k. these days."

"Oh, ya? Well, just don't start getting along too good." Sheila dropped her voice to a growl. "Or I'll stomp you until you're just dirt between my toes."

"Good God, that's awful! Have you been hanging around with a bunch of bikers or something?"

"Nope. Just made it up. Like it?"

"No." I glanced at my watch. "I'll see if Bonnie needs some help, then I'd better get to the game." I leaned over to give her a quick hug, but it turned into a long one, and I could feel tears on her cheeks.

"Are you o.k.?"

She nodded, but I knew her face was screwed up. She took a couple of deep breaths, then leaned back and smiled as well as she could. "Ya, I'm o.k. You have a good game, Steady."

Bonnie came in balancing a pizza in one hand and lugging a bucket of cleaning supplies in the other. "Hi, guys. How's it going?" Bonnie's quick, dark eyes appraised us. Sheila looked away, wiping her eyes and nose with a tissue.

"Pretty good," I said. "Cripes, why do you tempt me with a pizza? I can't eat before a game."

"There isn't enough for three anyway. Maybe we'll put aside some crusts for you."

"Thanks. I'll see you after the game, Sheila."

Bonnie said, "Hey, Kinkaid, I've got a tail light out. Can you take a look at it?"

"Sure."

God, it was cold. I leaned into the trunk of Bonnie's car and wiggled wires experimentally. "It's the one on this side," she said, plugging the bulb in expertly. "I knocked it loose when I got out the cleaning stuff. There, now it's grounded." I looked at her in disgust. She smiled wryly. "Sorry, I should have let you find the problem. I keep forgetting about male egos. Look, I just wanted to get you alone to ask how she's doing."

I started to glance toward the window, then stopped myself. I leaned in under the trunk lid, making a show of working. "She was kind of depressed, but then she got talking about acting and modeling and stuff, and seemed in a real good mood. But when she hugged me good-bye . . . I don't know. I think she realized that all the acting business is just a dream now. She started crying then."

"Ya, I kind of thought something like that'd happened. Where's the old lady?"

"Playing cards or getting drunk, I guess."

"Maybe I'll try to pump Sheila a little about her grand-mother. Something weird is going on."

"You got that right. Look, I've got to go." I slammed the trunk lid. "I'll talk to you later."

"O.k." She started for the house. "Earn your letter."

I took that as a shot and snapped, "I'll try, Tiger." She hesitated, then kept going.

129

I didn't earn my letter. The ball squirted through my hands and out of bounds four times in the first half. After that, Burke used Haz as a substitute. We lost.

I felt like hell. About the last thing I wanted to do was go to Sheila's, especially with Bonnie there to tell me whatever the radio announcer had said about my play. Still, I'd told Sheila I'd be back. Maybe I could make it quick. Complain that I had a headache or something.

Not a chance—things had gone to hell while I'd been away. Bonnie was at the sink doing dishes, her face fierce with anger. "What happened?" I asked.

She fired the dishrag at the opposite wall. "The old lady came home drunk, then laid into Sheila because there was no booze in the house! Jesus, the things she said. Sheila's in her bedroom crying. The old lady stumbled out, headed for the bar down the street."

"Oh, crap," I said, and started for the bedroom.

"Sheila doesn't want you to see her crying. She told me to send you after her grandmother. If the old bitch falls out there, she's going to freeze to death."

"No shit."

"I only got a little out of Sheila, but here's the story. Mrs. Porter is a boozer. She's been one for years. Sheila's been keeping her pretty straight, but now the old lady's fallen off the wagon. And if you point out that's a cliché, I'll punch you out, I'm so goddamn mad!"

"Take it easy, Tiger."

She brushed a lock of hair back from her forehead and sighed. "I just can't believe the crap she said. I mean, she blamed Sheila for being sick, then accused her of letting the place go to ruin as if the old lady was a cripple and couldn't do a damn thing for herself. Sheila ran, I mean just ran, into her bedroom, holding on to her stomach where they cut her. The old lady said something about 'weak little bitch' and walked out."

For a second I thought Bonnie was going to burst into tears. I took a step and put a hand on her shoulder. "Come on, Tiger. Just take it easy."

She put a hand on my arm for a few seconds, then turned away. I let my hand drop. She went on quietly, "I went in and talked to Sheila. That's when I found out about the old lady's drinking over the years. They've kept it pretty quiet by living like hermits. The old lady goes to her card parties, but she never invites anyone here. There are no relatives, no minister, just Sheila and her grandmother holed up alone. . . . Anyway, Sheila told me that stuff, then said she wanted to rest. So I came out here to do the darn dishes. . . . Do you think you can handle getting the old lady out of the bar?"

What the hell did I know about this kind of thing? I was no shrink, no social worker. "I guess if I have to."

"You're tougher than I am. I think I might lose it and try to kill her."

"I'm tempted. Call Phil at the bowling alley and ask him to meet me at the bar. This may take more than just me."

Outside the tavern, I sat in the car and smoked a cigarette from the pack I'd stashed in the glove compartment. Tougher than the Tiger—that was a compliment and a half, but I didn't feel very tough. Well, here goes, I thought.

The place was scuzzy. Heads turned my way, most of them belonging to old people whose faces showed evidence of heavy-duty drinking. Mrs. Porter was at a table in the corner, staring into a glass of beer. The bartender moved my way, his eyes suspicious. "Ah, hi," I said. "I know I'm underage, but can I get a Coke and talk to the old lady in the corner?" He looked her way, then got me a Coke. "A friend of mine is going to be here in a few minutes. We don't want Mrs. Porter walking in this cold, so we're going to try talking her into a ride home with us."

131

"That's your problem, bub. I just serve the drinks."

"Ah, right." I went over and sat down across from the old lady. "How you doing, Mrs. Porter?"

She stared up at me blearily. God, she looked terrible. "Not too bad. How 'bout you?"

"O.k., I guess. I came by to see if you needed—"

"Get me another beer." She shoved her glass toward me.

Well, maybe she'd come willingly after a free beer. She didn't thank me when I set it in front of her. We spent a few minutes in silence. Where the hell was Phil? "Ah, look, Mrs. Porter. Sheila's kind of worried—"

"I don't wanta talk 'bout her." Her voice rose. "If you wanta, you can just get outta here."

An old guy stood up from the bar and weaved over to us. "Is this kid botherin' you, Maggie? Want me to throw his ass out?"

"Na, he's a good boy, Larry. My gran'daughter's boyfriend. She sent him becuz she don't think her ol' granny can handle a couple of drinks."

The old guy looked at me. I had him by twenty pounds, four inches, and something like a half a century. "Well, you just mind your manners, boy. We don' take no botherin' of ladies here."

"Ya, sure," I said. He went back and crawled up on his bar stool.

Mike came in the door and surveyed the room with his dark, Indian eyes. He gave me a wave and bought a Coke. "Hi, Jerry. Hello, Mrs. Porter." I looked at him questioningly. He winked. "A sore back and Lisa; I volunteered to come instead. So how's it going, Mrs. Porter?"

She seemed to notice him for the first time. "You some kinda Indian or some other kinda foreigner?"

Mike grinned. "Indian, ma'am. Chippewa."

She looked back into her glass. "I like you people. Always

132

have. Understand how you feel losin' everything to a buncha greedy punks. Just like me. They took my daughter, and they give me a no-account gran'daughter to raise. And then they took my husban' and left me all alone. Had to move outta my home and rent a shack. Ain't fair. None of it was fair." Mike kept grinning. "Then you know what they done? Stuck me in a hospital for a month and said I couldn't drink no more. And they got my stupid gran'daughter to believe 'em. Little bitch. And now she's sick and gonna leave me too."

I felt my face get hot. "It isn't Sheila's fault she's—"

"Well, it sure ain't mine! I done the best I could for her!"

From the bar, Larry gave me a threatening look. I took a deep breath. "Look, Mrs. Porter, no one's saying—" Mike nudged me under the table, and I shut up.

Mike said, "I'm going to get another. How about you two?" Mrs. Porter drained her glass and shoved it over. Mike winked at me and brushed a finger against his lips. He came back with a deck of cards, two Cokes, and a beer from the low-alcohol tap. "How about a game of smear for a quarter?" Mrs. Porter looked up with interest. "Tell you what, since I'm not only the best but the luckiest card-playing Indian around, I'll match a six-pack against your quarters." That did it as far as the old lady was concerned.

Mike dealt. I passed. Mrs. Porter studied her cards. "I never get no cards, but I ain't going to let the dealer have it for two. I'll bid three."

"Must be better cards than mine," Mike said. "Go ahead." She led, and he let her have his jack for a point. The old lady cackled. I caught on to Mike's plan and played to lose. In ten minutes she had her fifteen points. "Well," Mike said, "the medicine ain't always right. I'm done for the night. Can I give you a ride home, Mrs. Porter?"

She stood, wobbled, and got her balance. Mike bought a

six-pack of low-alcohol beer at the bar. "Not that shit," the old lady said. "The good stuff." Mike shrugged.

We got her in Mike's car, and he drove her to Sheila's. When we got her to the door, he handed me the six-pack. "I'm going to take off. I don't want Sheila to be embarrassed. You know, Indian scout doing a good deed, then disappearing into the sunset. Got her, Kemosabe?"

"Thanks, Mike. I appreciate it. I'll buy you a belt or something."

He laughed. "No payment necessary. We don't work that way. Take care."

Bonnie was cool and professional as she guided Mrs. Porter to the bedroom. I checked on Sheila. She was curled up asleep, a wad of damp tissue lying next to her limp hand. I pulled the covers over her and returned to the kitchen. I lit one of Bonnie's cigarettes. She was back in ten minutes. "Did you smother her with a pillow?" I asked.

"Felt like it." She took a beer from the six-pack.

"She's going to notice that."

"No, she's not. You're going to take the rest with you. Whose stupid idea was it to lure her home with beer?"

"I don't think it was such a stupid idea." I explained the situation.

Bonnie nodded. "Ya, I guess you're right. You had to get her home somehow. Cripes, for somebody as smart as I am, I sure say stupid stuff sometimes. Like telling you to earn your letter tonight. I meant that to mean 'Have a good game.'"

"I didn't take it that way. I'm sorry."

"Don't say you're sorry. It's just my way of saying stuff. . . . Come on, drink a beer. Break training. You earned it."

I opened one. "What are we going to do?"

"We're going to get Sheila out of here, that's for damn sure. I think Mom will let me bring her home."

134

"I don't think Sheila will go along with that."

"We'll have to convince her. Let's take her to breakfast in the morning. Get her out of the house for at least that long."

"Bonnie, do you have any idea what you're getting into? I mean you'll be bringing a very sick person into your home. That's going to be real tough."

"I know, but what else is there to do? Well, I'll think about it." She took her beer and cigarettes to the table. "Do you have anything to read? I'm going to stay here tonight."

"I've got *Lord of the Flies*."

She winced. "Well, I guess I can read it again."

I got the book from the car and came back in. "Thanks," she said. She hesitated. "You know, you're all right, Kinkaid. I mean it. I'm sorry for some of the crap I've laid on you. Especially trying to hit you that day."

I felt awkward. "Well, no damage done, I guess. Thanks, Bonnie. You're o.k. too. Maybe I'll even stop calling you Tiger."

"No, don't do that. It makes me feel tough. I need that sometimes."

I didn't feel like going yet and chanced a question. "I asked before, but you never answered. Why do you care so much for Sheila? I mean why are you guys friends, anyway?"

Bonnie shrugged. "It's kind of funny. When I first got assigned to tutor Sheila, I absolutely despised her. I mean, here's this raving beauty who's got everything I ever wanted. She's tall, blond, athletic, and charming. Everything I'm not. And she's obviously smart enough, but she's too lazy to study. I kept thinking, 'Hey, blondie, what are you trying to pull? Just make it on looks and charm? Well, it ain't going to make it with me. I am going to work your butt off.' And I did. God, she hated it, but I kept after her. And all the while I studied her. You know, kind of a zoo-

135

logical investigation. I figured, 'Hey, I can't be like her, but I can at least understand her. Maybe pick up some of her tricks.'" She shrugged. "Before I knew it, I found myself liking her. And she liked me. So I dropped the zoological investigation crap and decided I'd just go ahead and be her friend. . . . That doesn't exactly put me in the best light, does it?"

"Well, not in the worst either, I guess."

Bonnie smiled wryly. "Ya, maybe not. . . . Hey, get out of here, huh? Get some sleep. I'm going to crash after breakfast tomorrow, and you're going to have the load with Sheila and the old lady for the rest of the day."

"O.k. You ought to get some sleep too."

"I will. I just need to sit up for a while. I'm used to it; I've spent a lot of Friday nights reading until two or three."

For a second I felt like saying, "Well, damn it, Tiger, if you'd just loosen up a little, maybe you'd get asked out on Friday nights." But I didn't.

At breakfast, Sheila looked good, her eyes bright, her skin rosy from the cold. She laughed at Bonnie's suggestion. "No way am I going to move out. Granny will be fine; we both just had a rough night. This has happened before. She'll feel guilty as hell today, and I'll have a long talk with her. Then we'll be back to normal. You guys worry too much about me. Let's talk about something else." She looked eagerly out the window of the coffee shop.

Bonnie stirred her coffee slowly. Her hair was mussed and her clothes wrinkled. "Sheila, you're sick. You shouldn't have to worry about your grandmother or keeping house."

"I'm not that sick!" For a second she looked angry, then grinned at us. "Hey, in a couple of weeks, they're going to give me the first dose of that medicine. By spring, I'll be fine. Stop worrying."

I tried. "Well, maybe you should just go to Bonnie's for a couple of weeks—"

"I'm not going to talk about it, Jerr-o. Forget it— Hey, there's Nancy Jo and Sue." She waved at a couple of girls through the window. They waved back, but kept going. "Shucks, I wish they'd come in. Well, come on, I want to go shopping. Buy some new jeans for this streamlined behind of mine." I glanced at Bonnie. She shrugged. Well, so much for Sheila moving out, but maybe she knew best.

Sheila hardly tired on the shopping expedition.

We'd delayed another meeting on the letters issue until after finals, but the following Monday we couldn't avoid it any longer. I think both Bonnie and I hoped that our recent friendship might help move things along. It didn't. The other committee members groaned when we stated the same old positions—not that any of them had anything better to offer. After an hour of beating on each other, we adjourned.

Bonnie caught me in the hall. "Let's quit."

"Huh?"

"I mean it. You and me, let's quit. We're part of the problem, not the solution. If we resign, maybe the rest of them can come to some sort of agreement."

I looked at her suspiciously. "What's the trick?"

"Honest to God, no trick."

I studied her eyes. "Hey, Phil!" Phil turned halfway down the hall. "Come here and listen to this."

He listened to Bonnie, thought for a second, then said, "I think it might work. I'm willing to try anything right now."

"Will you call the next meeting and tell people?" I asked. "Then you can elect a new chairman and perhaps caucus to work out new positions. If—"

"I'll figure it out," he said, grinned, and sauntered off.

137

Bonnie said, "Well, he didn't have to seem that happy about it."

"Ya, it makes you feel like you're about as worthless as—"

"Teats on a bull."

We laughed. "We're a team," I said.

TEN

The pain doubled Sheila over at the waist. I held her. When she could straighten up, her face was wet with tears and sweat. "Sheila, that's it. It's getting worse; we've got to get you to the hospital."

"It's just gas, Jerr-o."

"Bull. Now come on. I don't want to force you."

We drove in silence. Sheila winced and leaned forward, pressing her hands against her stomach. And I hurt deep for her.

The last week had gone pretty well. Mrs. Porter was off the sauce and doing her best to help around the house whenever she wasn't at the senior citizens' center or one of her innumerable card parties. Sheila grew stronger, and sometimes I forgot how sick she really was. She refused to admit that anything was happening inside her that the cancer drug wouldn't cure as easily as aspirin chased a headache. This evening she'd even planned to come to the basketball game. I prayed, hoping someone was really up above the cold winter sky: "Don't make it too bad, God. Give her a break for a change."

Dr. Belke joined the emergency room doctor, and they examined Sheila. I called Bonnie. She swore, then said, "I'll be there as soon as I can. Keep the faith, Kinkaid."

I waited. Thank God for the Tiger. We really *were* a team—not exactly buddies, but we could work together. Our arrangement had settled down to a routine. Bonnie came in the late afternoon to keep Sheila company and help with supper. When I showed up in the evening, Bonnie would gather her stuff and leave with a "Keep your mitts off her, Kinkaid; she's still healing," or something of the sort. I usually had a reply ready—we understood each other.

A nurse came out of the examining room. "The doctor is going to admit her to the hospital. He'd like you to get Mrs. Porter." This again. Well, I was used to it by now.

Sheila had been right: the pain was gas. But it wasn't a question of taking a couple of tablets and spending a little time downwind and out of earshot of other people. The operation had irritated a section of intestine so it now stuck together, trapping gas from escaping. Dr. Belke told us they could probably "decompress the bowel" by pumping the fluid from her stomach. He explained how they'd insert a tube through her nose, down her throat, and into her stomach. Even the thought of it gave me the creeps. Mrs. Porter stared at him with dim understanding.

It was almost evening before they allowed Bonnie, Mrs. Porter, and me into Sheila's room. She didn't greet us, but lay staring at the ceiling. A plastic tube the diameter of a pencil ran from her nose to a humming machine the size of a bedstand. Two bottles hanging above it were slowly filling with green fluid from her stomach. "Look at me," she said softly. "Just look at what they've done to me now." She grimaced in pain, squeezing my hand tight. "God, what I wouldn't give for a good fart. . . . My hand hurts too." She stared balefully at the IV line running to the back of her other hand.

"Maybe the flow is too strong," Bonnie said. "I'll get a nurse to check it." She left.

"Jerr-o, I feel like hell."

"I know."

"No, you don't know!" I sat silent. Sh squeezed my hand. "I'm sorry, Steady. I'm just so damn mad. I thought I was getting this thing licked, and now here I am again." Tears welled in her eyes.

What could I say? I'm sorry . . . I'm disappointed too . . . Be patient? I just sat there holding her hand. A nurse came in with Bonnie, smiled, said nurselike things, adjusted the IV, and left.

Bonnie nudged me and tilted her head toward the corner. Mrs. Porter had her eyes closed, and her lined, old-lady cheeks were damp. Bonnie went over, knelt by her chair, and talked quietly.

"Would you like to watch some TV?" I asked Sheila.

"No."

Bonnie turned. "Your grandmother's awfully tired, Sheila. I think it would be best if Jerry took her home on his way to the game."

The game! I glanced at my watch. The JV game had been under way for fifteen minutes. I stood up hastily. "I really don't have . . . Ah, ya, o.k. That's a good idea. I'll see you later, Sheila."

Sheila held on to my hand, then let it drop. "Sure. Later."

God, the old lady was slow. She spent a long time getting up, then standing at the end of Sheila's bed as if she wanted to say something, but couldn't. Finally, she followed me. She didn't so much walk as creep down the hall to the elevators.

In front of her house, I jumped out and opened her door.

141

She sat staring straight ahead. "I'll walk you to the door, Mrs. Porter."

She didn't move. "They're going to take her away from me. Just like they did all the others."

"Ah, this isn't a big deal, Mrs. Porter. That machine will take care of the problem in two or three days."

"Away," she said. "Just like all the others."

She wasn't going to move! I hesitated, then reached in and took her gently by the arm. "Come on, Mrs. Porter. Things will look brighter in the morning."

We were halfway to the door when she stopped. "I'm supposed to play cards tonight."

Will you just let it go, you old bat? "Well, maybe you could skip it tonight."

"There won't be enough to play. They'll be mad at me." She turned and marched resolutely back to the car.

I got to the bleachers with ten minutes to go in the JV game. Burke glared down the line at me, then turned his eyes back to the action. "Where have you been?" Phil asked. "Burke is superpissed."

"Sheila," I said. "She's back in the hospital."

Gary nudged me. "Coach says to meet him in the locker room."

I got up. "Good luck," Phil said. Gary gave me a swat on the butt.

I gave Mike a halfhearted grin when I passed him. "Got a tomahawk I could borrow?"

He smiled. "Forgot it at home. Sorry."

Burke was behind his desk. "I'm sorry, Coach. My girlfriend has been kind of sick—"

"I don't give a damn about your personal life, Kinkaid! You're supposed to be here for the JV game and that means from the start of the JV game."

"I'm sorry, Coach, I—"

"And in case you haven't noticed, I'm the coach of this goddamn team, not you. I've taken a lot of crap from you, Kinkaid. Like that little stunt a few weeks ago with Bowker. Don't think I didn't know who was behind that. Why didn't you have everybody stand up tonight? Give you a little welcome? Show everybody in the stands that this team ain't run according to the coach's rules, but Jerry Kinkaid's?"

I stood staring at the floor. Not only was the man an ass, he was a paranoid ass. I felt his eyes boring into me. I cleared my throat and looked up. "I'm sorry, Coach. It won't happen again."

"You're goddamn right it won't happen again. Next time, you're off the team. Tonight you're going to sit the bench, young man. Sit clear down at the end. And if seven guys foul out, you're still not going in. I'll play with four." He paused to recheck his arithmetic—let's see, twelve take away seven leaves five and with Kinkaid on the bench, I've got four on the court. Right, o.k. Now what was I going to say to the little bastard? "If you want to stay on this team, you're going to have to shape up, mister. No more lollygagging, talking to girls, and staring at the clock, you hear?"

"Yes, sir."

"And the next night we have a game, I expect you to be the first one here, not the last."

"Yes, sir." The door to the locker room opened and the rest of the guys started filing in. Burke got up and walked into the main room to start his pregame pep talk. I followed in a few seconds, looking suitably contrite. Mike winked at me, Gary grinned, and Phil gave me a thumbs-up when Burke wasn't looking.

Sheila was lying with her eyes closed. Bonnie was sitting close, reading a magazine. When she looked up, I beckoned. We went down to the lounge. "How is she?" I asked.

"Very angry. Very depressed. Every time one of the nurses comes in, she bites at her."

"How about the pain?"

"It seems a little better. You get to the game o.k.?"

"The old lady slowed me down." I told her what Mrs. Porter had said about losing everybody.

Bonnie stared out the window. "She's going to crack. Sooner or later maybe we all will. . . . So how'd the game go?"

"We lost sixty-seven to fifty. The usual."

"Did you do o.k.?"

"I didn't play. Burke benched me for missing the JV game."

"I'm sorry; I should have told you to get going earlier."

"That's o.k. You're not my keeper— Oh, shit. I forgot I was supposed to give Melissa a ride to the game. Just what I need, another person pissed at me." I sat down. "God, I hate to take crap from an idiot like Burke. I should have told him to stick it."

"Screw him. Forget it. . . . I can't handle any more tonight. I'll see you tomorrow, huh?"

"Ya, sure."

I sat holding Sheila's hand for a long time. She didn't say anything, but slow tears of anger and frustration oozed from the corners of her eyes. After the nurse told me I had to go, I kissed Sheila. "Be patient," I said.

"Right," she whispered. "There's all that eternity waiting."

I couldn't think of anything to say. I kissed her again. "I'll see you in the morning."

Mom was waiting for me, and she was pissed too. "Jerry, Melissa was very upset. She couldn't find anyone to take her

144

to the game, so she woke me up, and I drove her in. Now I'm a little upset, because I didn't get enough sleep and have to go to work tired."

I apologized and explained what had happened.

"Well, you should have called her, Jerry. There must have been a few minutes to do that."

"I know, Mom. I'm sorry."

She paused, then sighed and put her hand across the kitchen table to touch mine. "Jerry, I worry about you, dear. You're so caught up in this thing. Sheila's a nice girl, but you can't let this ruin your life. Melissa called from her friend's and said you didn't play tonight—that you were benched or something."

"I got to the JV game late. Burke was mad, but it'll blow over."

"Jerry, you've got to keep things in perspective. You've got your studies, basketball, your friends, and the two of us. I know Sheila means a lot to you, but you've got to keep some balance in your life."

I laughed, and it sounded odd, almost crazy. "It's funny, Mom, because a few weeks ago, Sheila didn't mean much to me at all. We'd had fun, but I'd gotten kind of tired of all her antics. I was going to tell her that we should try going out with some other people. Like you said the night she broke the chair: maybe I'd enjoy someone with a serious side. But then this happened. . . . And it doesn't get any more serious than this." My voice caught, and I put my head in my hands. "So what can I do but see this through?"

"But, dear, it may be months before she recovers completely. And she's got her grandmother. You can't expect yourself—"

"I don't know if she's going to recover, Mom. The doctor isn't holding out much hope. And Mrs. Porter—hell, she's in the way more than anything."

After a long minute, she said quietly, "There are some things you haven't been telling me."

"I didn't want you to worry, Mom. You know, make you feel like you had to help out." She nodded and waited for me to unload.

When I finished, she got up to pour coffee. She laughed wryly. "Darn. Now I'm going to go to work feeling guilty after bawling out my son for trying to be heroic."

"I'm no hero, Mom. This whole thing scares the crap out of me."

She sat. "I know it must. . . . When Sheila gets home again, maybe I can get over to do some of the cooking and cleaning."

"No, Mom. That doesn't take much time. It's the being with her, and Bonnie and I can't really pass that off on anybody else." She nodded and glanced at the clock. "Go ahead, Mom. I'm o.k. I'll talk to Melissa when I pick her up."

Mom got up and gave me a hug. "Sure, she'll understand."

Melissa was cool when I picked her up midmorning. I took a deep breath and started explaining what had happened with Sheila and later Burke. After a minute, Melissa pulled up her knees and started crying. "Hey, don't cry, Mel. You had a right to be mad. I should have called, but things got, you know, kind of balled up."

She let herself go for two minutes, then wiped her nose and eyes. "I should have guessed something was wrong. You looked so upset during the game."

"God, I hope it wasn't too obvious."

"To me it was. But I was still mad at you. I spent all afternoon doing the chores around the house without any help. And then when I had to wake Mom so I could get to the game . . ."

"I know, Mel. I'm sorry. I haven't been pulling my share of the load." I glanced at my watch. "I'll try to do some stuff before going to the hospital."

"You don't have to."

"I should."

"No, you shouldn't! Take care of Sheila. I'll do the chores. I can at least help that way."

I looked at her and felt suddenly like I was seeing a grown-up person, not just my twirpy kid sister. "Thanks, Mel. I can use some help right now."

We drove for a while in silence. "Jerry, is she going to get well? I mean, is there any chance?"

"I don't know, Mel. The last few days, I thought she was getting a lot better. The doctor said that stuff about 'very grave,' but maybe he was wrong. Once she can have that drug, maybe she'll be o.k. I try to keep my hopes up— Oh, hell, look what the plow did." The town plow had been by, leaving a foot and a half of gouged snow and ice ridged across the mouth of our driveway. I pulled the car to the side of the road. "We'll have to shovel."

We got shovels from the garage and attacked the snow. At least this was a problem we could do something about.

A nurse disconnected the pump so we could walk in the hall for a few minutes. Sheila pushed the IV stand with one hand while I kept a light hold on her other arm. She brushed angrily at the eighteen inches of loose tubing hanging from her nose. "Gross," she muttered. I couldn't think of anything funny or consoling to say, so I kept my mouth shut. A woman pushed a cart of full lunch trays past us. Sheila looked at the food longingly. "After three days, at least they could let you have soup or something. Cripes, all I've got is hunger cramps now."

A nurse helped her back into bed and got the pump reattached. Sheila punched the button on the TV remote, rejecting show after show. "Come on," she muttered, "show me a little class." She paused on a station showing the "High School Quiz Bowl." "Here's one for you, Jerr-o. Lots of details."

"I'd rather watch basketball."

"I'd think you'd get enough of that; you're always gone practicing or playing."

I'd been ignoring her shots for three days, but this one got through. "Horseshit. You know that's not true."

She glanced at me, then away. After a moment, she said, "I know it's not. I just miss you when you're gone."

I looked down. Shouldn't have sworn at her. "Ya, I know. I'm sorry I snapped at you."

She swallowed hard. "I had it coming."

Bonnie poked her head in. She was dressed in her Volunteen uniform. "Hi, guys. Sue and Becky are on the way up. Back in a minute."

Sheila grabbed a hairbrush from the bedside table and began furiously brushing her hair. The IV tube got in her way, and I stood to hold it at a more convenient angle. "Crap," she muttered. "I hate surprises. How do I look?"

"Fine."

She held up the tube running from her nose, then dropped it in disgust. "Oh, what the hell. Showtime. I read Sarah Bernhardt used to do it with a wooden leg. I guess I can do it with a tube in my nose."

"Who was Sarah Bernhardt?"

"Greatest actress of all time. God, I guess you don't know all the details."

"Guess not." I waited, hoping the girls would hurry.

It bugged me that more of Sheila's friends hadn't come to see her. During her recovery from the first operation, only two or three had bothered. Not much had changed this time, although Mike had surprised me by wandering in

148

Sunday afternoon when both Bonnie and I happened to be in the room. "Couldn't score you any magic mushrooms, so I threw this together with some junk I found in the garage." He handed Sheila a complex knot of feathers and leather that looked vaguely like a human figure. "It's supposed to be a talisman, but I guess we ought to call it a taliswoman. Heavy medicine, lady."

Sheila grinned. "Thanks, Mike. I need all the help I can get."

He sat down to talk, and Bonnie and I slipped down to the lounge to burn one. "Why aren't more people coming to see Sheila?" I asked.

Bonnie didn't reply for a moment. "I'm not sure, but I don't think Sheila's been really close to a lot of people. Except you, that is. And me, I guess. She's always been just a little too different for most people. . . . Anyway, I'm going to talk to Sue and Becky. I think they'll come."

"It'd buck her up."

"Buck her up," Bonnie mused. "Haven't heard that one in a long time. Where *do* you get all these snappy sayings?"

"I have to think about something when I'm sitting on the bench during a game."

"Everybody's got to have a hobby, I guess. . . . I wonder where Mike got the talisman."

"Don't you think he made it as a joke?"

"I doubt it. Mike's too serious about his culture. I'll bet it's something that's been handed down in his family."

"But why should he give her something that means a lot to him? Hell, they barely know each other."

"I think they know each other enough. Mike's a very perceptive guy, and he knows we're losing somebody pretty special." Suddenly, the Tiger had to turn away and take a deep breath to get control. "Sheila's never given a damn about surface stuff. Mike's an Indian. So what? I'm a stuck-

149

up, brainy bitch. So what? You're a handsome, arrogant jock. So what? She cared about what was inside of us. Made us her friends. . . . And I'm talking about her like she was already dead!" The Tiger turned tear-filled eyes on me, then spun and hurried out.

Bonnie had damn near cracked that afternoon, and I was getting close to it now. I left as soon as Bonnie brought Sue and Becky into Sheila's room. Outside the hospital, I lit a cigarette automatically, got my car started, and drove aimlessly for a few blocks. How much longer could I take it? I needed a blast of cold sanity or maybe a little craziness. I stopped at a gas station and called Phil. "Come over," he said. "I've been looking for an excuse to get out."

We drove out into the country north of Junction. The night was cold and clear, a billion stars throwing dim light on the wind-hardened snow in the fields. "You won't believe this place Lisa and I discovered," Phil said. "There's this old, raunchy dude running a little grocery store with a four-stool bar. He doesn't have a license to sell beer, but does it anyway. Says the liquor laws are unconstitutional. We might as well enjoy it while it lasts; he'll get busted one of these days."

"I hope it's not tonight."

"Chance you take. Turn right up here."

Albert's Outpost was definitely strange. Jammed in a single room were a couple of coolers, a few shelves of canned goods, a pool table, four stools, and the damnedest collection of fishing baits and novelties I'd ever seen. The backbar was plastered with right-wing bumper stickers. Albert served us both without a second glance, then went back to staring at the TV. "So what's the news?" Phil asked me.

I told him, a little surprised at the bitterness in my voice when I mentioned the absence of Sheila's friends. I broke it off. "I've got to take a leak."

Phil grinned. "The best part of Albert's—the can is outside."

"You're kidding."

"Not a bit. Don't fall in."

I used the outhouse. Albert's Outpost was definitely going to get shut down—and soon. I wondered if the old guy would drag out his shotgun to hold off the police and health inspectors.

When I came back in, a big, heavyset girl was standing with her back to me, talking to Phil. She turned, a sleeping infant cradled in her muscular arms. "Well, hi, handsome."

"Oh, hi, Maureen. How are you?"

"None too shabby. How's yourself?"

"Getting by, I guess." I sat, feeling awkward. "Want a beer?"

"Wish I could, but I've got to get the kid home to bed." Albert emerged from the back room with a bag of potatoes and put it beside a gallon of milk. She paid him. "Hope to see you guys around." She winked at me and left.

"Nice girl," Phil said. "A tad on the large side."

"Ya, a little bit."

"Say, did she turn your eyeballs around that night? I don't think I ever asked."

"Close, but we stopped a little short of it."

"Hmmmm. . . ." He seemed to remember that we'd been talking about Sheila only a few minutes before. "Hey, Albert, could we get a couple more over here?" Albert delivered the beers.

"Phil, why don't you come by and see Sheila one of these days? She'd like that."

"Ya, I should."

"You keep saying that, Phil, but you don't. How come?"

"I don't know, man. I'm busy, and . . . Oh, hell, I don't know. It's just sick people. I've never been comfortable around sick people."

151

Suddenly, I was very angry and not sure exactly why. "This isn't just a sick person, Phil! This is Sheila."

"Ya, I know. I'll make it up there."

"Give me a date."

"One of these days."

"Goddamn it, Phil. Not just 'one of these days.' Give me a date!"

He set down his glass very carefully. "Don't push me, man. You ain't got the right or the muscle."

"Do you want to walk home?"

"No. Do you want to fight?"

"No, damn it, I don't want to fight. I want to know when you're coming to see Sheila."

"O.k., tomorrow! I'll come and see her tomorrow. Now just back off!"

"You boys wanta fight, go somewhere else." Albert didn't turn his gaze from the TV.

We sat in silence for a couple of minutes, not looking at each other, then Phil leaned forward. "Look, I'm sorry this has happened to you. I'm sorry it's happened to Sheila. But you're obsessed with it, man. You let her run your life when she was healthy, and now she's running your life when she's sick."

"That's not true."

"Well, I think it is. Now just listen to me for a second. We're in our junior year in high school. Do you ever listen to those seniors talk? 'Ya, my junior year was the best. Ya, that's when I really had fun.' Maybe they're full of shit, but do you know what senior year means to me? Reality time. Time to figure out what you're going to do with the rest of your life. So this year I'm partying. I'm going to play ball, study enough to get by, and beyond that I'm going to drink just as much beer and screw Lisa just as many times as I can. That's what concerns me right now. Now I'll come up and

152

see Sheila, but don't expect me to get involved like you and Bonnie Harper have. I just don't have the time. Do you understand?"

I looked into the hard intensity in his eyes. "I thought you were a better friend than that."

He slapped two dollar bills on the bar. "Well, maybe that's where you were wrong. Albert, could we get two for the road?"

"None for me," I said.

"These two are for me. You do what you want."

We rode back to Conklin in silence. I think we both felt like hell about the fight, but there didn't seem to be anything to say. Phil didn't go to see Sheila the next day.

ELEVEN

A kid I didn't even know slipped me a note near the end of practice on the afternoon of Sheila's fourth day in the hospital: "Get up here quick. Bonnie." I didn't dare leave: Burke would kick me off the team surer than hell. I stayed the last fifteen minutes, skipped my shower, and ran to my car.

At the hospital everything seemed normal. Sheila lay asleep, the pump beside her bed humming softly. No one at the nursing station seemed upset about anything. A tall nurse looked up from some paperwork long enough to hand me another note. It read: "I'm in the cafeteria. Bonnie."

The cafeteria was nearly empty. Bonnie sat at a table in the corner, slowly stirring coffee, a wisp of her dark hair clamped firmly in the corner of her mouth. I pulled up a chair. "Hi, what's the crisis?"

She brushed back the hair from her cheek and looked at me. Her eyes were red. "They had to hold her down, and I helped. . . . Damn, that's no way to start." She looked

155

down and took a deep breath. "The pump didn't do the job, so Sheila's got to have another operation. That means four or five more days without food or water and three more weeks before they can give her the first dose of that cancer drug. Sheila told them to go to hell, that she wasn't having another operation, and that she wanted the drug right now. When the doctor said that wasn't possible, Sheila said she was leaving and started pulling at the tube from the pump. They stopped her, and she went crazy, biting, kicking, and hitting. They held her down until they could get a tranquilizer into her. I tried to help, but then her grandmother was at the bed, trying to say something, trying to calm Sheila down, just . . . just trying . . ." Bonnie started crying. "Shit."

I reached out a hand. "Tiger—"

She waved my hand away quickly. "No! . . . No. I'm o.k. Just give me a second." She drank coffee, trying to regain control. "They told me to get Mrs. Porter out of there, and I did. Then a couple of minutes later she disappeared. Just walked out while I was trying to find her a cup of coffee. Now she's probably somewhere getting drunk." She choked back a sob. "And I wish I was with her!"

Bonnie sat with a hand over her eyes, tears sliding down her cheeks. I felt numb, helpless. After a long minute, she whispered, "I just can't stand all this pain. Cripes, even I can't be a bitch all the time."

"You're not a bitch, Bonnie. You're about as—"

She turned away, rummaging in her purse, her voice suddenly stronger. "Just don't talk to me right now, huh? Go back upstairs. I don't want you to see me like this."

"It's o.k."

"No, it's not!" She found a tissue and wiped her face savagely. "I can't afford it."

"Hell, Tiger, you're human."

"That's the problem." She got up quickly. "I'm going to clean up." She spat out the next few words: "Put on the game face, as you jocks say. I'll see you upstairs. We've got to figure out how to handle this."

As it turned out, we might as well have saved our time. Sheila didn't need any convincing. In the morning, she was grim and determined. "Let's get this over with quick. Slice me open, repair my guts, and get me back healing. I need that drug. It's all these goddamn details I don't need." She reached down under the covers and scratched. "And my pubic hair was just growing back. Now they're going to shave me again. Crap."

When a nurse came in to give her the preoperation tranquilizer, Sheila snapped, "I don't need that. I'm as tranquil as I'm going to get."

"Doctor's orders."

"Screw him," Sheila muttered, but rolled on her side to get the shot. The nurse smiled.

They did the operation late Thursday morning. I went to school, trying to make as many classes as I could. Then practice. "She'll be groggy," I told myself, "and Bonnie will be there as soon as she can." That didn't help much, and I had a lousy practice. A kid from the JV team stole the ball from me twice, and I couldn't make a shot go down to save my ass. I could feel Burke watching me with a cold stare. On the sidelines, Phil shook his head and looked away after I made a particularly bad pass.

I sat out our win against Bridgman Friday night.

For days after the operation, Sheila lived on the IV tube and rage. Before the operation, she'd snapped; now she snarled. Any nurse or aide who entered the room risked losing a piece of anatomy. A minister who tried some

157

friendly comfort learned that in a hurry when Sheila yelled she'd call security if he didn't get his ass out of her room.

I wasn't expecting a pleasant greeting when I was late getting to the hospital the Tuesday after the operation. I paused in the corner near the elevators to burn a quick one. Sue and Becky Roberts, Sheila's friends, came down the hall leading from the ward. Becky was crying. "Why does she have to be so mean?" I stepped back, and they didn't notice me.

This has gone far enough, I thought. I crushed my cigarette and headed for Sheila's room. Sheila was glaring at the TV. "Close the door," she said. "It keeps the damn nurses from staring at me."

I closed the door. "I saw Becky and Sue in the hall. You must have said something to upset Becky." Sheila shrugged. I sat down. "I think people might visit more often if you were a little nicer to them."

"I don't care if they come or not."

"Don't hand me that, Sheila. You care a lot."

"No, I don't."

"Bull."

For the first time she turned her head to look at me. "So what am I supposed to do? Make jokes? Put on one of my little acts? Hey, it's all right, folks. Don't worry—Sheila's only dying. But, by God, she's got a funny skit to show the lighter side of cancer." She sat up and held an imaginary microphone to her mouth. Her voice tensed. "O.k., folks, watch closely now. The incision has been made, and the doctors are slowly pulling out Sheila's guts. It seems they've found something underneath. Yes, they definitely have. I think one of our spotters may be able to see it now." She held her hand to an imaginary earpiece. "Yes, yes. Folks, it's a tumor! Let's hear it for Sheila's tumor! Wait a second, some more information is coming through. The tumor is the size of a—Anybody want to guess? O.k. you, the lady in

the front row in the orange tent dress. Speak up, please. . . .
She's right, folks! Sheila's tumor is the size of a *footbaalll!*
How about that, folks? You can sit down now, ma'am.
We'll have some gifts for you after the show, including our
new record, 'Jokes for the Terminally Ill.' Now—"

"Stop it, Sheila."

"What's the matter? Isn't this funny enough? Hold on,
there's more." She put her mouth close to the imaginary
microphone. "Now back to the action, folks. They're cutting out the tumor. We'll be able to see it in a moment.
They say it's got an odd color, almost a sure sign of cancer.
There! It's out! One doctor passes it to another, he passes it
to a third. Oh, oh, one of the nurses is breaking downfield.
It's the old option pass! The tumor's in the air. . . . She's
got it! What a catch!"

I lunged for the bed, my vision blurry with rage. "Goddamn it, Sheila! Stop it!"

She clapped both hands over her face and let out a wail. I
stared disbelievingly at my uplifted hand. For a long moment, time seemed suspended. Sheila slid down in the bed
and lay sobbing. I turned and sat in the chair by the window, staring numbly at the frozen world beyond the hospital. After two or three long minutes, I said, "I'm sorry,
Sheila. I didn't mean to scare you. I wouldn't have hit
you. . . . But I just couldn't stand it anymore. Cripes, you
can't put people through stuff like that."

She reached for a tissue, then lay staring at the TV.
"Come sit by me, Jerr-o," she whispered. I moved close and
held her hand. "I'm sorry," she said. "That was horrible. I
knew it when I was doing it. But sometimes—" She started
to cry again. "Sometimes I just can't live up to what people
expect. Not when I'm so scared because they won't give me
that drug, and all I can do is just lie here thinking about that
cancer growing in me. Just think and think while it grows
and grows until sometimes I think I'm going to go crazy!" I

159

put my arms around her, and she cried for a long time. Finally, she quieted. "We're in this together, aren't we, Steady?"

"Ya, all the way."

"Just stick with me, huh?"

"Sure."

I spent the next couple of days trying not to think too much. Just hold on, I told myself. Once we get her home, she'll be calmer. And when they can start the chemotherapy, maybe she'll start getting well. Just hold on. Ride it out.

Mrs. Porter was sober and seemed to have the schedule for the afternoon firmly in mind. As soon as Dr. Belke gave the o.k., she was supposed to help Sheila check out, then call Bonnie to come pick them up. Cripes, even Mrs. Porter should be able to handle that. I parked at the hospital entrance, got her into the lobby, then rushed back to the house to help Bonnie clean.

She was scrubbing the kitchen counter when I came in. I pulled off my coat. "Hi, Tiger. How bad is it?"

"Better than before. A couple of empty wine bottles and about a case of beer cans in the trash out back, but at least the old lady made an attempt to clean up."

"Good; I don't have much time. The bus leaves for the game in Oleron in an hour." I opened the refrigerator to stick in the pie Mom had sent along. "Cripes, where'd all this stuff come from?"

"The old lady's card partners, I think. I guess somebody finally figured out they could use some help over here. I wouldn't worry about finding space for the pie; it doesn't have to be refrigerated."

"Oh, right." I put the pie on the counter and dug around in the refrigerator. "Some good-looking stuff." I helped myself to a plate of sandwiches. "Sheila's got to start eating more. She bitched all the time they wouldn't let her eat, but now she hardly eats at all. Cripes, is she skinny. She must be down another ten pounds."

I turned from the refrigerator. Bonnie had a queer look on her face, but only said, "Do you think you can mop the kitchen floor?"

"Sure, piece of cake."

I expected her to give me a jab for the cliché, but instead she went into the living room to straighten up. As I ran water into a pail, I realized that Bonnie hadn't said much to me in the last week even when she'd had the opportunity. I called into the living room, "Hastreiter twisted his ankle in practice last night, so I'm number one sub again. At least I think so."

"One way to get your job back."

"Well, I don't think I should have lost it in the first place." She started the ancient vacuum cleaner.

She came back into the kitchen when I had the floor mopped and the dishes washed. She said, "You might as well take off; I can handle the rest."

I glanced at my watch. "I can stay a few more minutes."

"No, that's o.k. Get going." At the door she said, "Ah, Jerry . . ."

"What?"

"Nothing. Have a good game."

"Wait a second. What were you really going to say?"

She gave me a long look. "It's about the food, Jerry. Don't kid yourself; Sheila's not going to eat much of it. She's not going to gain back the weight she lost."

"Well, I think her appetite was a little better last night."

Bonnie half turned away. "Look, Kinkaid, just don't do this to yourself. Don't start taking Sheila's hopes seriously."

"But the drug could work."

"That's a chance in a thousand. Maybe a million. The cancer is all over her insides." She swallowed, then turned back to face me. She spoke carefully. "It's o.k. to hope for a

161

miracle, but just don't let her hopes set you up for a really big fall." We stared at each other. "Just don't do that to yourself. . . . Now get going before you're late. I don't want to be blamed for that."

"Ya, sure. I'll see you tomorrow."

On the bus, Phil said, "Hi," but sat down a couple seats behind me and started shooting the bull with a kid from the JV team. Mike took the seat across from me, smiled faintly, and closed his eyes. "You look like hell," I said.

"Flu," he said. "Custer's revenge. I shouldn't have come." He fell asleep.

I rode alone, thinking about what Bonnie had said. Had I started kidding myself recently? Maybe, but then again . . . To hell with it. I wanted to feel good for a change. I worked my fingers, then imagined the ball in my hands. That was the motion. Come on, Coach, put me in. I've got the touch.

Burke had to pull Mike five minutes into the first quarter, and I hit the floor with big plans. I was terrible. One second the ball felt half-inflated, the next second it was squirting out of my hands. Usually, we got chewed up inside, but now I couldn't even get the ball in to Gary and the forwards. After one bad pass sailed out of bounds, Phil whispered fiercely, "Cripes, Jerr, get with it, huh? We beat these guys last time." Next time downcourt, I took a shot so wide of the mark that a couple of guys on Oleron's team laughed. We were down by 10 at halftime, and it was mostly my fault.

Burke was screwed, and he knew it. Mike spent halftime in the john with the runs, and Haz hadn't even suited up for the game. The guards behind me were scrubs, guys so bad that they didn't have a quarter of playing time among them. Burke took me aside. "What the hell is the matter with you, Kinkaid?"

162

"I don't know, Coach. Nothing's working."

"Well, make it work! Get your mind in the game. You play five more minutes like that, and I'll put in Peterson." Peterson? Cripes, he was the worst of the worst. Had I fallen that far?

Gary told me to stay loose, and Mike slapped me on the butt as we went out to start the second half. Nothing I'd told myself at halftime made a damn bit of difference. Two more bad passes and I was on the bench for the night. Oleron blew us away.

In Conklin, I got off the bus with my head down. A hand fell on my shoulder. Burke pointed to my bag. "Anything in there personal?"

"Ah, just my jock."

"Take it out and give me the rest. You're off the team, Kinkaid."

"Coach, I did the best—"

"The hell you did! You haven't played worth a damn in weeks. Give!"

Numbly, I handed him the bag and stood holding the limp jock in my hand as he marched toward the locker room. Fury grabbed me, and I started after him. "Don't. The son of a bitch isn't worth it." Mike was standing a dozen feet away. "Come on, let's talk." He led me a few paces from the bus.

The other guys had been watching. Gary and Phil were talking now. Gary gestured angrily, then followed us. Phil hesitated, then trailed behind. The others drifted closer. We stood together, no one saying anything for a moment. "We'll go on strike," Mike said. "If we stick together, Burke will cave in."

"Right," Gary said, and a few of the others agreed. Phil looked at his shoes, then nodded.

I took a deep breath of the winter night—felt anger,

163

relief, and desolation all at the same time. "It won't work, guys. He's a coach, and they always win." Mike started to protest. "Screw it, Mike. He's right: I haven't played worth a damn for a long time. To hell with it." There was silence. "Thanks anyway, guys, but I just don't need B-ball anymore. We'll see you later. Cripes, Mike, go home, huh? Get some sleep."

I walked to my car, feeling them watching me, then starting to disperse. In the Dodge, I reached into the glove compartment for a cigarette. Well, no need to hide the smoking anymore. For a second tears stung my eyes. I blinked them back and got the car started. O.k., now what? Go see if Sheila was still awake? Even the thought of it made my stomach turn over. Not tonight! Damn it, I didn't need to go every night. I slammed the car into gear and put the accelerator down hard. The tires spun and grabbed.

A block from the school, I had it planned out. It was time to *get down!* I stopped at the gas station where the night guy sold what I needed, then used the pay phone.

"Did you finally get drunk enough to call me?" Maureen laughed.

"No, I haven't had a drink. But I plan to fix that."

"Well, come over. I've got what you need."

A couple of times on the way to Junction, doubts crawled into my head, but I slapped them down. It was not my goddamn fault Sheila was dying. I'd done my share to help out, but this bullshit of being a nice guy had gone far enough. Time for some craziness. Maureen had what I needed—beer and a lot more. Things that Sheila had never given me.

I followed Maureen's directions to the far side of Junction. The house was small, the paint flaking off the sides. Maureen swung the door open before I could knock. "Hellooo, handsome." Inside the house was warm, cozy.

She held a finger to her lips. "The kid woke up a few minutes ago. I think he's asleep now, but we've got to be quiet."

She led me to the kitchen and got two beers from the refrigerator. I put out a hand to take one, but she said, "You gotta earn it," and laid a long kiss on me, her pelvis thrusting into mine, her large breasts flattening against my chest. She leaned back, her eyes dancing. "God, I didn't think you'd ever call. Come on, we'd better sit down and drink a beer, or I'll scare you away."

"No chance," I said.

We sat on the old couch and drank beer. She ran her fingers across the back of my neck. "Might give me some advance warning next time; I had to do three days' cleaning in half an hour. No time to wash my hair either."

"It looks fine."

"My house or my hair?"

"Both."

"You look pretty nice too." She reached for me, and we didn't talk for ten minutes. Finally, she pushed me away. "Were you a good Boy Scout? Come prepared?"

"Ya, I did."

"Good." She pulled down her sweater. "I've got to use the bathroom before we go any further." She was back in a couple of minutes. "Want another beer?"

"Ya, that'd be good."

From the kitchen, she called, "Well, I know what we're going to do the rest of tonight. Maybe tomorrow night my sister can take the kid, and we can do some dancin'. I'm a mean dancer." She danced back into the living room and handed me a beer. "What do ya say?" She flopped onto the couch and put her legs across my lap.

"Well, depends where we go."

"What's wrong with the Purple Horse? Suits me fine." I hesitated. Shit. I couldn't think of a plausible lie. The silence lengthened, and her eyes narrowed. She swung her feet off my lap and lit a cigarette. She drew deep and exhaled slowly. "Well, you'd better tell me."

I thought desperately, but there was nothing I could really tell her except the truth that because of Sheila, I couldn't be seen with her. Feeling about as low as anyone could get, I told her. She listened, staring at the surface of the coffee table. After I finished, there was a long silence before she said, "I see." She drained her beer in two long swallows. "That's quite a story. Calls for another beer." When she sat down again, she raised the can. "Well, cheers."

"Maureen, I'm sorry. I should have told you."

"That's o.k. I don't expect too much from men. You can't when you look like me."

"I like how you look, Maureen. It's just—"

She waved a hand. "Don't bullshit me. I'm just trying to figure out if my feelings should be hurt."

"I didn't mean to hurt you. I just needed someone, you know. I mean, that doesn't sound right, but—"

"Don't dig yourself in any deeper." She smoked and thought for a long minute. "Ya, well, I've decided my feelings aren't hurt." She looked at me and smiled. "I'm kind of complimented that you'd come to me when you were so down. I got a chance to dream for a while and that was nice. Thanks for not lying tonight and dumping me tomorrow. That would've hurt."

"I shouldn't have come. It was a lousy thing to do to you . . . and to Sheila."

"It's o.k. You didn't hurt me. And I ain't going to judge on anything between you and your girlfriend. Nothin' in my life gives me the right." She reached back and fastened her bra. "I guess you'd better go, Jerry."

I felt sick. Sick in a dozen different ways for a dozen

different reasons. At the door she kissed me on the cheek. "Good luck," she said. "Maybe I'll see you someday."

Outside, depression hit me like a hammer. For a second, I almost turned back, ready to beg for a little time, a little comfort, just a two-hour hug and nothing more. But it wouldn't work. Couldn't work. She'd probably deck me with the nearest heavy object. And maybe I'd welcome it.

I drove back into Junction. Stay cool, I told myself. You're depressed and a little drunk. You can go home and be more depressed or go to the Purple Horse and get more drunk. The choice was obvious, but it was nearly midnight, and I'd have to work fast.

I didn't sit with anyone I knew, but found a corner with some Junction kids. When a bottle got passed to me, I filled a third of my glass. The owner raised his eyebrows. "That's a two-dollar drink, man."

"Make it three," I said, and poured more.

News had traveled fast. In the next half hour, three kids from school stopped to ask about me and Burke. I gave them all the same answer: "I'm off the team. That's all I want to say."

Ten minutes before closing, I weaved my way through the crowd and out the door. Bonnie was leaning against my car. "I'm driving," she said.

"Hey, Tiger. How's your sex life?"

"Can it. Give me the keys."

"Jerry-boy's o.k. Don't sweat it."

"The hell you are. Come on, give me the keys."

"Screw you, Tiger. I said I'm o.k."

She stepped forward—no fear, just cold anger. "Look, there's a cop car out by the road. You make the smallest mistake and your ass is grass."

"Sounds like a cliché to me."

"Shut up. You'll lose your driver's license, pay one hell of a fine, and maybe end up in juvenile court. Do you want that on top of everything else?"

I hesitated. I felt like saying I didn't give a shit what happened, but even in my foggy brain, I knew I did. I handed her the keys.

I had to tell her to stop on the way back so I could get sick beside the car. I got back in and closed my eyes. God, I felt awful. A couple of miles farther on, she asked quietly, "Why did you do this to yourself? Everyone in the place knew you were drunk out of your skull."

"I don't know. There's just so much shit coming down right now, I had to do something. . . . Did you hear I got kicked off the team?"

"I heard."

"And the hell of it is, I had it coming. With all this crap about Sheila, I haven't been playing worth a damn."

There was a pause as she passed a slow-moving car. "Well, you made an ass out of yourself, but I guess I can understand. It's hard on me, but when it's someone you love—"

For some reason, I blurted it out. "Hell, I never loved her. I was going to break up with her."

She turned her head quickly, then said softly, "Oh, my God."

At my house, she was brusque. "I'll bring your car back in the morning. Make some excuse to your mom about having to lend it to me."

"Ya, right."

I started to get out of the car, but she put a hand on my arm. "Take care of yourself, Kinkaid. We'll make it. We're the team that counts. . . . Enjoy your hangover." She put the car in gear.

———

I was on my knees, leaning into the toilet bowl, when Melissa came to the door of the bathroom. "Are you going to be o.k.?" Her voice was small, frightened.

"I'll survive." I puked again.

"Sounds like you'd rather die."

"I would. Mel, please don't tell Mom. Just this once." I heaved again.

"Is there anything I can do?" I shook my head. "I won't tell," she said.

She got my bathrobe and draped it over my shoulders.

TWELVE

Melissa poked her head in the door. "Mom just called. She's going to work some overtime."

"Thank God." I moaned and put my head under the pillow.

"I could make you some breakfast."

"Don't even talk about it."

"Well, I'll be around. Oh, your car's back. Bonnie and her Dad dropped it off twenty minutes ago."

"Good." I tried to go back to sleep, but memories of the night before came fast and hard. God, what a jerk I'd been. I rolled over and looked at the clock on my desk: eight-thirty. I had to get up; Sheila would be expecting me soon.

I accepted some juice and toast from Melissa and tried not to watch as she wolfed down bacon and fried eggs. She let me know that she expected some details about my evening in exchange for her silence. Well, fair was fair, and I gave her a rough outline, omitting any mention of Maureen. It hurt her to hear I'd been kicked off the team—having a big brother on the varsity had been a pretty big deal for her—but I gave her credit for trying to be sympathetic. She agreed to break the news to Mom.

We sat at Sheila's kitchen table. I'd given her just enough details to explain why I looked and felt like I was dying. "Poor Jerr-o. I've sure screwed up your life, haven't I?" She reached out to brush hair back from my forehead.

If I'd been truthful, I would have said, "Yes, you sure as hell have," but I didn't. "No, it was nobody's fault but my own."

"Well, at least you won't have to worry about basketball, and we can be together more." I only nodded. She paused, then said, "I'm glad Bonnie kept you out of trouble. You two sure get along a lot better these days."

"Ya, she's o.k."

She gave me a long, searching look, then got up from the table. "Come on, you need a nap."

We lay in her darkened bedroom. I put my arm around her and closed my eyes. Through her bathrobe, I could feel the outline of her ribs. She said, "I should have asked you in here when we both felt better."

"That would have been nice." Let me sleep, I thought.

She was quiet for a long minute. "I'm still your steady, aren't I, Jerr-o?"

"Of course you are. Don't give me any of that crap about wanting to make a move on Bonnie."

"Just wondering."

"For God's sake, don't."

I was just about asleep when she said, "Next Friday is Valentine's Day. Will you take me out?"

"Sure, if you feel up to it."

"I'm going to. Sheila Porter needs a big night on the town."

I shifted my weight, mumbled something about "the bigger the better," and fell asleep.

Mom called in the afternoon. "Melissa and I are bringing over a spaghetti dinner around five."

"You don't have to, Mom. There's lots to eat here."

"I want to see the situation firsthand, Jerry. The spaghetti is an excuse."

There was no sense in trying to talk her out of it. I said good-bye and told Sheila. She was a little flustered, but warmed to the idea. We called Bonnie and asked her to join us for supper.

Dinner went fine. Mrs. Porter didn't say much, but ate well. Sheila ate what she could. Mom and Bonnie kept the conversation moving with Melissa chipping in for all she was worth.

I stuck around for a while after Mom and Melissa left. When I got home, Mom was sleeping for her shift at the mill. A note lay on the dining-room table: "Jerry, now that I've seen the situation for myself, I realize that you've got to carry through with this thing. Melissa and I will give you all the support we can. Maybe next fall you can get back on the basketball team, but I don't think you should worry about that now. Also, dear, I think you should take it easy when you're away from Sheila. Go for a walk or find someone to talk to. Phil or Gary or me. Someone. (Bonnie seems a bright, understanding girl, no matter what you've said about her in the past.) I don't think drinking a lot of beer will help. And, son, try not to smoke so much. There must be a dozen empty packages under the seat of your car. Anyway, tell me if there's anything I can do to help, and remember you have our support and love. Mom."

Melissa was watching me. "I didn't tell her," she said. "Somebody else did or she guessed."

I nodded. "It doesn't matter. It wouldn't take Einstein." I looked through the window into the February night. "Want to go out and get cold?"

173

Melissa didn't hesitate. "Sure. Maybe it'll improve my complexion."

Even if Sheila's fantasies of a quick and complete cure came true, she'd missed too much school to complete her courses. She happily gave up any pretense of doing schoolwork. For a few days, she tried the latch-hook kit Bonnie had brought, but it bored her. Dreams and plans were Sheila's specialties, and she spent long hours talking about the big Valentine's Day celebration.

She wanted a new dress for the occasion, and Mrs. Porter roused herself long enough to do the sewing. Bonnie helped with the fitting on Friday afternoon. Mrs. Porter had used Sheila's old dimensions, and the dress hung from Sheila's shoulders and ballooned around her waist and hips. The old lady looked stricken, but Sheila seemed delighted with the dress. "Oh, take it up a little here, a little there. It's not the package, but what's inside that counts." Bonnie and Mrs. Porter did their best.

Sheila got bored standing on the chair. "Hey, hurry up with the details. My steady and I got big plans."

"Just let me put in a couple more pins," Bonnie said. "There."

Sheila spun on the chair. "How do I look, Jerr-o?"

The truth was not good. The red of the dress turned her skin white, and the clinging fabric made her look almost skeletal. "Great," I said. "Take it easy on that chair; I've already fixed one."

"Always worrying." She hopped down awkwardly. "Come on, Granny, help me get this off." I wandered into the kitchen.

Bonnie joined me. "God, that red couldn't be worse. It makes her look like a corpse." She lit a cigarette, her fingers shaky.

"Are you o.k., Tiger?"

"Ya, sure. Why shouldn't I be?"

"Just asking; we haven't had much of a chance to talk recently."

She leaned against the counter, one arm across her middle as if her stomach hurt. "I'm o.k. No problems. How about you?"

"All right. It took me two days to get over that hangover, but I'm being a good boy now. Thanks for saving my butt that night. I don't think I could have kept it on the road."

"You're welcome. I'm sorry you got kicked off the team. I know it meant a lot to you."

"I'll get over it." There was a pause. "Are you going over to Sue and Becky's party later on?"

"No, I don't think it'll be a scene for girls without dates."

"Oh, I bet there'll be lots of kids by themselves. Besides, we'll be around."

"I already see you two more than I want to." I must have looked hurt at that, because she smiled ruefully. "No offense intended. . . . Anyway, I'm scheduled to volunteer at the hospital until late."

Mrs. Porter returned to the living room with Sheila's dress. Bonnie stubbed out her cigarette and went to help sew the alterations.

The evening was a disaster. The dinner at Cordoba's cost me plenty, but most of Sheila's steak went into a doggie bag. The movie had a lot of action, but Sheila dozed off. A lot of people at Sue and Becky's party made a big deal of her, but she got flustered. She cried on the way home. "I just don't have it anymore, Jerr-o. I can't eat; I can't stay awake; I can't deal with people. And I look like a scarecrow. I'm done. I'm all finished."

"Stop it," I said. "You did fine for the first time out in a

175

while. People understand you're not feeling up to par. It'll be better next time."

"There's not going to be a next time."

"Don't talk like that," I said, but I knew she might be right. I'd seen her out with healthy people now, and the truth was beginning to sink in.

That evening took something out of Sheila. Maybe it was hope, maybe it was just her ability to go on fooling herself. She talked less, cried more. I tried to interest her in stuff: books, games, TV, school gossip, even her old fantasies about becoming a famous actress. Nothing worked for long. I had to be careful—if my frustration came through as anger, she'd start crying, and I'd feel like crap.

Since I didn't have B-ball practice anymore, I started coming some late afternoons, while Bonnie started taking some evenings. I preferred afternoons, since the old lady was usually gone somewhere, and I didn't have to watch her sitting forlornly in front of the TV or fumbling around trying to be of help. At least she wasn't drinking, as far as I could tell.

There wasn't much to do in the afternoons until time came to start supper. I'd do homework on the kitchen table, while Sheila sat staring out the window, an unread magazine or the untouched latch-hook kit in front of her. Sometimes I'd catch her looking around the room with tears in her eyes. If I asked what bothered her, she'd turn away with an angry shake of her head. Maybe I should have pressed her harder.

The ruptured vacuum cleaner bag lay in the doorway to the kitchen. Sheila sat crying in the dust strewn across the living-room floor. I knelt beside her. "Hey, it's o.k. I'll clean it up. Why were you worried about vacuuming?"

She didn't look at me. "It needed to be done."

"No, it didn't. Bonnie did it just a couple of days ago." I glanced around the room. Sheila had started half a dozen projects and not finished a one.

She waved angrily at the cloud of dust eddying around her. "And I'd just about finished the dusting."

"I'll do it again. It only takes a few minutes."

"For you, not for me!"

"Sheila, you don't have to worry about any of this."

"Yes, I do!"

I let her cry for a couple of minutes more, then coaxed her to the kitchen table and got her some 7-Up from the refrigerator. When I thought she'd settled down a little, I asked gently, "Sheila, what's going on? You know Bonnie and I can take care of the cleaning. We've been doing it for weeks."

"I've got to get off my fat ass and start doing stuff, Jerr-o! For years I've done everything around here for Granny. I can't quit now. It's when people stop doing things they die. Nobody ever died vacuuming a rug!"

I started to say, "Sheila, that's crazy," but stopped half-way and just stared at her. Her lips quivered. Then before I could stop her, she jumped up and stumbled into the living room. She threw herself down on hands and knees and scooped dust into the torn bag. All the rapid movement was too much for her, and she wobbled. More clots of dust cascaded from the bag. Then she was crying hard, kneeling in the dust. I held her and fought back my own tears.

Sheila dozed on the couch while I cleaned up and started fixing supper. When I was sure she was asleep, I picked up the phone and called Bonnie. After I'd finished telling her about the vacuum cleaner incident, she took a long time before saying, "Her grandmother is the problem. We've got to do something so Sheila can stop worrying about her."

"Ya, but what?"

"We've both got last hour off tomorrow. I think we ought to go over to Oleron and talk to someone at social services. We probably should have done it a long time ago. I'll ask Sue and Becky to come over for a while to keep Sheila company. Sue will anyway; she's tougher."

The social worker was a tall, dark woman with streaks of gray in her hair. Ms. Matthews listened to our description of the situation, watching us with cool but sympathetic eyes. I guess both of us must have been showing the strain. After ten minutes, she interrupted gently, asked a few questions, then shook her head slowly. "You young people have been trying to handle too much on your own. You're to be complimented, but someone from the hospital should have picked up on the home situation. . . . Well, that's not important now."

She glanced at her notes. "All right, social services can provide someone to clean the house. Nutritional advice and help in preparing meals can be provided. If the situation calls for it, we can recommend a full-time housekeeper. Now all this is going to cost money, but you say that Mrs. Porter seems to have some income." We nodded. "I'll call on Mrs. Porter and Sheila tomorrow afternoon about three to see what services are desired. Can one or both of you be present?"

"I can be," Bonnie said.

Ms. Matthews checked back through her notes. "I think that's all the information I need at the moment."

I guess that was the signal to thank her and leave. We didn't move—one more question had to be asked. I cleared my throat and heard myself ask it in a voice that seemed distant, no longer entirely my own: "What happens after Sheila dies?" For an instant, I felt Bonnie's hand on my arm.

"I'll arrange appropriate services for as long as Mrs. Porter is able to stay at home. Eventually, it will probably be more practical for her to move to a nursing or adult foster home. I'll explain those options to them."

Outside the building, Bonnie said, "As simple as that."

"Ya," I said. "As simple as that." Neither of us spoke again until we were well on the way back to Conklin. "Tiger," I said, "maybe we have tried to handle too much, but I don't want to quit now. Having a cleaning woman a couple of times a week would show Sheila that social services will take care of her grandmother. But I don't want any more help than that. I don't want some stranger taking over everything." I turned to look at her. "We've gone this far; I think we should see it through with Sheila . . . all the way to the end."

I'd never seen Bonnie's eyes so dark, so deep. "Yes, we're in this all the way. You, me, and Sheila. Hey, watch the road!"

"Oops, sorry. Then you'll tell Ms. Matthews that's the way we want it?"

"Yes." She settled back and lit a cigarette. We watched the road come on in the falling darkness. I glanced sideways at her. She seemed to be smiling at something a little funny, a little sad.

Sheila's anger seemed to disappear after the visit from the social worker, but the tears didn't. For a week, she didn't do much but sit in the big easy chair in the living room with a box of tissues beside her. She said that the hard chairs in the kitchen hurt her bones, and it wasn't difficult to see why. Once she'd joked about becoming "svelte," but now she was thin, almost emaciated.

After coming home from the hospital, she'd counted off the hours until she could receive the first dose of the cancer drug. Now days crept by when she didn't mention it. The three weeks of waiting finally passed, and I drove Sheila and Mrs. Porter to the hospital. I tried to be cheery, as much for myself as them. After all, there might still be enough time for the drug to work. But Sheila seemed listless.

Dr. Belke examined her, then sent for us. "Sheila's recovery from the last operation has been slow; I think we should delay the medication another week."

Sheila began crying softly. "Do we have to?"

"It would be wisest," he said.

Sheila got up slowly and walked out. The old lady shuffled behind her, mumbling, "It's all right, dear. Just another week."

I turned to Belke. "Doctor, isn't there something you can do?"

He shook his head slowly. "I'm afraid not. If we'd caught the cancer six months ago, maybe the treatment would have worked." He lifted a hand, then let it fall back to the desk. "Now, the drug will only make her feel worse. And there is a danger of cardiomyopathy, damage to the heart muscle."

"But what's going to change in a week?"

"The chances are she'll be worse. There is a small chance she'll be stronger. Then we might risk the medication."

"Why do you keep talking about chances? I mean, there's no chance unless she gets the medicine! Why not just give it to her and see what happens?"

He fixed me with a long, steady gaze. "Because we do not want to increase her discomfort without reason." He studied his hands for a moment. "I don't want to tell you that there is no hope. Cancer is a mysterious disease. Sometimes there are unexpected and inexplicable remissions. But in Sheila's case, with or without the drug, it is extremely unlikely that the situation will improve."

I took a deep breath. "Then how long . . . ?" My question hung in the air, unfinished.

"No one can be sure. My feeling is not long—that's as specific as I can make it. . . . I'm sorry. I wish I had a miracle in my bag, but I don't."

On the way home, I asked Sheila, "How about some ice cream?"

She shrugged slightly. "I guess I could try."

I drove over to northern Wisconsin's only year-round drive-in. The winter had begun to ease, and the carhops had abandoned their snowmobile suits for regular winter coats. Jill Odegaard, one of our classmates, came to my window. "Hi, Jerry." She leaned down so she could see Sheila better. A look of alarm passed over Jill's face, but she managed a big smile. "Hi, Sheila. How's it going?"

Sheila didn't look at her. "O.k."

"Well, what can I get you guys? For Sheila it's on the house. Hey, we really miss you at school, Sheila." Sheila didn't reply. I ordered for the three of us. Jill whispered, "I can do better than that. Just watch."

What arrived with the simple sundaes for Mrs. Porter and me was the biggest and most exotic banana split ever made in Conklin. Jill grinned. "Enjoy." Sheila managed a smile. It was the best she could do on her last visit to the world outside the house, the hospital, and her dying.

The pains came again five days later when Sheila was home alone. She called me at school. I got to the phone in the main office out of breath from running halfway across the school. "I've got pain, Jerr-o," she said, her voice sounding distant and dull. "In my stomach. Same place as before."

"Call an ambulance. I'll meet you at the hospital."

"No, just come and get me. You don't have to rush; it's just the same old pain. See if Bonnie can come too."

"Are you sure you'll be o.k. until we get there?"

181

"Ya, pain's just a detail now."

I found Bonnie and we started the familiar routine: talk our way out of school; pick up Sheila; get her to the hospital; dig Mrs. Porter out of the senior citizens' center; and wait for the results of the exam and X rays. The news was bad. The tumor had grown back and now pressed against Sheila's intestines, blocking the path for wastes. Once more, the doctors would have to cut her open, carve away on her insides, then sew her back together again.

That evening Bonnie left to run Mrs. Porter home, and I sat with Sheila in the darkened room. She had a painkiller bouncing around in her system, and I hoped she'd sleep to gain strength for the operation. Instead, she talked, her voice odd, a little cold. "You know, I used to believe in God. When I was in the hospital the first time, I prayed a lot. Told God I'd be a good girl if he'd just let me live. The second time I was here, I got mad, told him he was a pretty cruel God if he couldn't give me a break. 'Hey, you. Put up or shut up with the loving God stuff.'" She paused, trying to keep it all straight. "Then last week, after I couldn't even change a bag in the lousy vacuum cleaner, I tried out the let-God's-will-be-done stuff. . . . But now I know that was just as stupid as all the other crap I'd tried. There just isn't any God, Jerr-o. Everything's an accident. We're all just a bunch of details flying around, bouncing off each other. And when you put all the details together, they don't add up to anything except a big pile of unconnected details. . . . What do you think of that, Jerr-o?"

What was there to say? "I don't know. Maybe you're right."

"I'm right. You'll know it someday when it's your turn to die. . . . Just think, Jerr-o, you'll probably be eighty-something, and I'll have been dead more than half a century. Will you still remember me, Jerr-o?"

My eyes were stinging. "Of course I will."

182

"Just think, you'll have been a husband, and a father, and probably a grandfather, and a successful game warden, or teacher, or something." The coldness in her voice snapped, and she sobbed, "And I won't have been anything!"

I tightened my hold on her hand. "You have been something, Sheila. You've made a lot of people happy, especially me."

Her hand stayed limp. "I didn't make you very happy. I didn't sleep with you at the resort like I kind of told you I would. After that I thought you were going to tell me it was all over between us. And I didn't know what I was going to say. I liked you a lot, Jerr-o, told myself I loved you and that maybe you loved me even though you didn't like saying so. But there were a couple of guys from the play who'd been calling me, and I just didn't know if I should choose one of them or let you make love to me so we could stay together."

I put my head down on the covers next to her and tried to hold back the tears. "But, Jerr-o, neither of them ever came to see me in the hospital. And you've been with me through the whole thing. Now I know you loved me even when I wouldn't sleep with you, that you would have stuck with me until I could say yes. You would have, wouldn't you, Jerr-o?"

I didn't know what the truth was anymore, and it didn't matter. "Yes."

She rolled on her side and pulled me to her with a strength I didn't think she had anymore. She was crying. "I'm sorry, Jerr-o. I should have let you that night. I was scared, and I didn't feel good, but I should have let you. I know it would have been good. And afterward you would have said you loved me without me asking." Suddenly, her right hand was fumbling with my belt. "We can still do it. Just close the door for a few minutes. Help me, Jerr-o!"

"Stop it, Sheila."

"No, I don't want to stop! I don't want to die without

loving you like I should have!" She had her hand half shoved in my pants, her fingernails clawing my skin.

"For God's sake, stop it!" I pushed her away hard.

She lay sobbing. "I'm still the same person, Jerr-o. I'm not pretty anymore, but I still love you." She covered her face with her hands.

I stared at her, unsure if I felt more love or horror. Automatically, my hand reached out to check if the IV was still in place. Then I put my arms around her. "I love you too, Sheila. Just take it easy. Just rest. What happened or didn't happen doesn't make any difference anymore. I still love you."

She cried herself out, and finally I felt her body relax. When I was sure she was asleep, I stumbled out of the room, past the nursing station, and through the door to the stairwell. I sat on the steps, my legs drawn up, my face in my hands. Bonnie found me there. I'm not sure who made the first move, but we held on to each other for a long time. All I could say was, "Goddamn it, Tiger. Goddamn the whole stinking world."

"I could have killed you."

Bonnie laughed, her cheeks pink. "I just felt so damn sorry for you after Dad gave you that lecture on how to jack up a car. Then you were so polite on the ride back while he was telling stories, and I knew you were mad enough to chew nails. I either had to laugh or cry. So I started laughing, but it wasn't at you."

"I see that now." We smiled at each other. "Want to split another Coke?"

"Sure." I got up and went to the vending machines. For an hour since a security man had chased us out of the stairwell, we'd been sitting in a corner of the deserted cafeteria. We'd been smoking cigarettes, drinking pop, and laughing

184

about all the times we'd been at each other's throats. It seemed odd, but it felt wonderful.

I got back to the table. "So, what other funny stories do you have?"

"Oh, I don't know. Maybe the time at the Purple Horse when we had to dance together after Gary cut in on you and Sheila. You dance better than I thought you would."

"Star athlete on basketball court or dance floor. Six of one, half a dozen of the other."

She grimaced. "God, I hate that one. Have you been using all those clichés just to irritate me?"

"Well, you seemed to enjoy pointing them out."

She laughed. "Ya, it was kind of fun." She reached out a hand to touch mine. "I'm sorry I've been a bitch so much of the time."

"I think it came out about even." I hesitated. "You know, I've always wondered why you tried to hit me that day."

She took her hand away. "I don't think we'd better talk about that right now."

"Why not? We've been talking about everything else."

"Why do you think I did it?"

"Cripes, I don't know."

"Take a guess then."

I shrugged. "O.k., if that's the only way I can get you to talk about it." I leaned back, thinking. "First I thought you were just crazy. Then I thought maybe you were just furious because you thought I might hurt Sheila. Just use her and dump her, you know. How close am I?"

"Not very." She poured Coke, watching it fizz. "What the hell, I guess it can't make matters any worse."

"What?"

"Just talking to myself." She folded her hands and stared at me. "It's a bad habit you develop when you don't have anyone to talk to a lot of the time." She absently twisted a

185

lock of hair. "Let me tell you a couple of things about me, Kinkaid. One, I'm a bitch, but you already know that."

"I don't agree."

"Well, I do a lot of bitchy things then. I'm hard on people. I've been hard on you." She took a breath. "Two, I'm seventeen years old, and I've never had a real date. I'm no raving beauty, but I'm not that bad, either. Still, no guys call. I'm smart enough to know why."

"Well, why are you so tough on people, Tiger? Why do you always have to make it so plain how damn smart and competent and tough you are? Why don't you just ease up a little?"

She grimaced. "God knows I've tried a few times. . . ." Suddenly, her eyes turned fierce. "But do you know what that makes me feel like? Like just another bullshit artist. I'm every one of those things you said I am, and I'll be damned if I'll hide it." She leaned forward, her right hand halfway across the table. "All I've ever wanted is for people to meet me on my own level. I like people with enough guts to stand up to me. . . ." Our eyes stayed locked for a long moment, then she pulled back and looked away. "People like you."

There was a pause. "I guess I don't see what all this has to do with you being so mad that day."

"Think about it," she said.

Suddenly, something snapped into focus for me. "Wait a second. You're not saying you were . . ."

"Don't laugh."

"I'm not laughing. And I'm not playing any more guessing games. Go on, tell me." She didn't look at me. "I'm meeting you on your level, Tiger."

She turned, her eyes blazing. "O.k., I was jealous! If you were taking any girl to a scumbag motel, I wanted it to be me, not Sheila! There, now you've got it! Now you can laugh. And I'm sure Phil and Gary and all the rest of your jock friends will think it's just hysterical!"

"Don't go paranoid on me, Tiger. They're not going to know. And I'm still not laughing."

Suddenly, her dark eyes were full of tears. She turned away quickly, brushing them away with a hand. She dug in her purse for a tissue. "Tough—what a lot of horseshit. I'm just as soft as everybody else."

We sat like that for two or three minutes. Scenes from the last few weeks flashed through my head. I'd missed all the signals, and there had been plenty. Finally, I asked quietly, "How long has this been going on?" She shrugged. "Come on, Tiger, you can trust me."

"I'm not used to trusting people. . . ." She blew her nose into the tissue, then turned around. Her eyes were swollen, and she didn't look much like the ferocious Tiger anymore. "Oh, hell, I don't know when I lost my mind. Maybe in the letters committee. I tried everything I could think of, and you wouldn't budge. God, I hated you for being so damn stubborn. . . . But I liked you for it too. A guy Bonnie Harper couldn't run over. Then when we helped Sheila practice for the play, I saw you really did care about her. That you weren't just some jock out for a quick piece of ass. . . . It got worse after that. I thought about you all the time, but I didn't know quite why at first. Then when I took that swing at you, it got clear real fast. Cripes, Bonnie Harper insane with jealousy over a guy who didn't even like her, who wouldn't think about taking her out in a million years."

She took a breath. "I really did hate you then, and I decided I'd go on hating you. Just beat down all my silly emotions by hating you. But, cripes, then you go and turn out to be somebody pretty damn special: You're spending all your free time with Sheila. You're cleaning her house.

You're doing all sorts of things that no ordinary guy would do." Her voice cracked, and she started crying again. "God, why did you have to turn out to be such a nice guy!"

"There are a lot of things you don't know, Tiger."

She waved away my words. "Just save it. Let me finish wallowing in the emotional slime. . . . So I tried to avoid seeing you. And I was a cold bitch when I did. 'Just give it some time,' I told myself, 'and you'll get over this stupid crush which is probably all hormones and emotional strain anyway.' But that didn't work worth a damn, either. There was always Sheila to worry about. We had to talk and be together, and I just couldn't fight it off. It got so I hurt all the time. For a month it's been ridiculous. . . . Bonnie Harper in love. What a joke."

The connections in my brain just weren't working fast enough. After a long minute, I said, "I'm going to need some time to think about this."

She got up quickly. "Don't." She took a deep breath. "Look, I'm upset. I've said a lot of stuff I didn't mean. And it wasn't right for me to say any of it. Not right, immoral, stupid. Sheila is dying, and that's all that counts. Go home, have a good laugh, then forget we ever had this sloppy little conversation."

"Tiger . . ." I was talking to her back. I thought of following her, but I didn't.

I had to get my coat from Sheila's room. She was sleeping curled up, her mouth open, her breathing hoarse. I brushed a wisp of hair from her face, hair that had once been golden, but had lost its sheen with her sickness.

On the way home, I tried to get a handle on things, but it was no good. I sat at the kitchen table for half an hour before I went to the phone and dialed. A sleepy voice answered. "Warden Harper."

"Mr. Harper, Jerry Kinkaid. I'm sorry to call so late, but I need to talk to Bonnie."

"Jerry . . . ? Oh, ya. Sheila's friend. Just a minute."

Bonnie came on the line. "Tiger," I said, "I'm not going to forget, and I'm still not laughing. Give me some time, that's all." She started to say something, but I kept going. "I'm not going to hold you to anything you said. It's been a weird night after a weird couple of months. And, for God's sake, don't go on any kind of guilt trip about anything you said. Believe me, I've got a lot more to feel guilty about than you do."

"Like what?" she asked softly.

"I'll tell you about it some other time. Now look, Tiger. You were right: Sheila's all we can worry about right now. But later we'll figure out this other stuff. Is that a deal?"

There was a long pause. "Yes."

"One more thing. Don't ever try to convince me you're a bitch. I know it isn't so."

THIRTEEN

Sheila slept most of the first two days after the operation, awakening now and then to the morphine-dulled reality of her dying. The tumor had been only the size of a large marble, but Dr. Belke told us that the "seeding" of smaller tumors was "widely disseminated" on the bowel, the lining of the abdomen, and the liver. The doctors had spliced intestine around the blocked section of the bowel, but all their knives and skill couldn't stop the cancer. They'd stitched her up, leaving the cancer to eat her guts.

We waited it out with Sheila. Bonnie and I had our schedule and our deal. We exchanged news on the situation, but nothing else. Maybe we'd have something more to talk about in a few days or weeks. Maybe not.

Sue, Becky, Mike, Mr. Armstrong, and a few other people dropped in to see Sheila. She'd smile at them, say she was doing o.k., and usually drift back to sleep. Most people left in a few minutes, feeling they'd fulfilled their obligation. Only Mike ever stayed for a while after Sheila fell asleep.

The minister Sheila had bitten a few weeks before dropped in daily for ten or fifteen minutes. Sheila now smiled at him, although I am unsure if she found him a comfort or only vaguely amusing. He was o.k., never laying anything heavy on her. He'd talk for a few minutes about the weather, maybe tell a joke, then say a brief prayer before he left.

Mrs. Porter had recovered her equilibrium. She arrived by taxi in the mornings, sat dozing in Sheila's room for a couple of hours, then left before noon. Bonnie dropped in at the house a couple of times in the evenings, but found no evidence of heavy boozing or impending breakdown. "She was nice. We drank tea and talked about her card playing. I think she's done her mourning already."

"Damn nice of her to get it done early."

Bonnie shrugged. "Well, she's old. She doesn't have much time left for anything."

Crazy as it seemed sometimes, life kept going on. Mom worried about me, cautioned me again to keep some part of my life separate from Sheila's dying. I told her I was trying. Melissa did most of my share of the chores. We didn't say much important to each other, but I felt closer to her than I ever had before.

Sheila's cancer no longer amounted to big news around school, and few people asked about her regularly. I really didn't talk to many people about anything. I saw Gary and Mike some, but Phil only nodded when we passed in the halls. I missed his friendship, and I missed basketball—not so much the game as the feeling of being part of a team. Still, all that seemed a thousand years ago. Now there was just the numbing routine of seeing Sheila through to the end.

I couldn't do much except be with her as she drifted in and out of sleep. When she slept, I did schoolwork, read, or sat smoking in the lounge. When she was awake, I held her hand and did my best to keep a conversation going. God, that was hard. What could interest her anymore? I searched frantically for topics, even jotted notes to myself at school. But after a few minutes of trying to keep her attention on life, I'd be reduced to saying, "Well, I wonder what's on TV?"

In the middle of the week following her third operation, I was just about to reach for the remote control when Sheila whispered, "Jerr-o, we're still going steady, aren't we?"

"Sure. Steadier than ever, I'd say."

"I promised I'd never ask for it, but can I have your ring?" I nodded and worked it off my finger. She curled it in her fingers and lay holding it against her chest. "I won't need it long. Then you can have it back."

I had a lump in my throat the size of a hand grenade. I lowered my head and fought the tears. Then she was singing, her voice soft, but gathering strength.

> *"Teen Angel, woooo*
> *Can you hear me?*
> *Teen Angel, woooo*
> *Can you see me?*
> *Are you somewhere uuup above?*
> *And am I still your owwwn true looove?"*

I looked at her in amazement. She was laughing. "My God, that song's twice as old as you are," I said.

"An oldie and a baddie. Hush, I know more.

> *"What was it you*
> *Were looking for*
> *That took your life that night?*
> *They said they found*
> *My high school ring*
> *Clutched in your fiiingers tiiight.*

"Teen Angel, woooo
Can you hear me?
Teen Angel . . ."

She started coughing, caught her breath, and hummed the rest of the chorus, ending with a final, mournful "wooooo." She smiled at me. "Have I still got it, Jerr-o?"

"It was the best performance ever."

She grinned. "Thanks." She held out the ring. "Here. You can have it back now."

"Keep it."

"No, it was just a prop for the performance. A detail. I didn't need it before; I don't need it now. You were all I needed." She pushed the ring into my fingers, then ran her fingers gently through the hair at my temple. "Give it to someone else soon. Give it to Bonnie."

"Bonnie?"

"Sure, you guys would do o.k. together. Maybe better than we did. . . . We weren't very well matched in a lot of ways, were we, Jerr-o?" I didn't say anything. "But we had some laughs, huh?" I nodded. She lay smiling at me for a long moment, her fingers moving softly in my hair. "You look tired, Jerr-o. You stay around here too much. Why don't you go home for a while?"

"I'm o.k. I want to be here."

She closed her eyes, and her voice was dreamy. "I wish we'd painted that water tower purple. With pink and green stripes. God, it would have been beautiful. . . ." For a moment, I thought she'd fallen asleep, but she shifted her weight and opened her eyes. "That singing wore me out. I think I'll sleep for a little while. Give me a kiss, Steady. Just in case I don't wake up."

"Don't talk like that."

She smiled faintly. "Well, it's going to happen, Jerr-o.

194

Ain't many more details except the last one." I started to protest, but she said, "Hush. I need to rest."

She lived another week, but that was the last time I had anything much like a conversation with her. She woke, then slept again. They removed the tube from her nose but left in the IV. Dr. Belke checked her a couple of times a day, but he didn't wake her if she was sleeping. The nurses and aides slipped in and out. Bonnie and I traded off the waiting. Outside, the weather warmed, and winter started letting go.

Late one evening, Sheila was awake long enough to talk some to Bonnie. Bonnie told me about it later, puffing nervously on a cigarette to keep her tears back. "Sheila said something like: 'It's hard to think straight just lying here. I mean, they take care of you. You don't have to worry about anything. Kind of like when you're a baby, and your mother takes care of everything for you. Sometimes I think I kind of remember back before my mom got killed. Just memories of being warm and safe. I've always wondered what she was like. Maybe I'll find out.'"

Bonnie put a hand over her eyes. "Take it easy, Tiger," I told her.

I faced a long watch at the hospital on Friday, since Bonnie would be tied up until late evening with the annual volunteer banquet. After school, I spent a few minutes talking to my trig teacher, then went looking for the Tiger. I didn't have any particular reason to see her; I just wanted to talk a little. Her car was still in the lot, but I couldn't find her anywhere in the academic wing. I wandered down to the gym. Pep rallies weren't exactly Bonnie's kind of thing, but maybe she'd decided to have a quick look at the peasants getting worked up for the big game. The team had been playing way over its head for three weeks, and a victory over the conference leaders would qualify Conklin for the regional tournament. Incredible.

I scanned the bleachers for Bonnie as the cheerleaders belted out the old cheer for introducing the players: "Colburn, Colburn, he's our man. If he can't do it, nobody can. Bowker, Bowker, he's our man . . ." and so on through the starters. Pam Thompson was leading the others, and she must have had an old roster stuck in her head. She started on the reserves: "Kinkaid, Kinkaid, he's . . ." The other cheerleaders went silent. Pam's voice trailed off, and she blushed red. Some in the crowd laughed. I spun on my heel and walked out. Behind me, Pam got her act together and yelled, "Hastreiter, Hastreiter . . ." On the way to the hospital, I felt about as low as I could get.

Sheila woke in the late evening, and I did my best to cheer her with the school gossip. No luck. I turned on the TV. "Do you want to sit up a little bit?" She shook her head. Mike knocked lightly on the open door. "Mike's here. Do you want to talk to him?" She shook her head. "Well, I'll be back in a few minutes." She didn't reply.

We walked down to the lounge. "I'm sorry, Mike. She's kind of tired tonight."

"It's o.k." I lit a cigarette automatically when I sat down. "White man make smoke," he said.

I glanced at the cigarette and grimaced. "Ya. It's kind of something to do."

"You ought to quit those things. They'll kill you."

"Can't say I really give a damn right now." He didn't say anything, but sat watching me. "So how'd you guys do?" I asked.

"We lost. Could have had them in the fourth quarter, but Gary fouled out on a bum call." He shrugged. "After that, it was the same old story."

"Did you have a good game?"

"Not bad. Stole two, got four or five assists and six points. 'Bout average. . . . Bad deal this afternoon. Pam was about ready to leave for Brazil after the pep rally."

"I'll get over it."

We sat in silence for a minute or two. "So how are things going up here?" he asked.

"Not so hot. She doesn't eat anymore. She sleeps most of the time. And when she's awake, I can't think of much to say to cheer her up."

He looked down at his hands. "Ya, I stood by the door listening for a few minutes. Scouting the territory, you know. Old Indian trait." He thought for a moment. "Why are you saying anything at all?"

"What am I supposed to do? Just sit there?"

He got up and stood looking into the night. "Ya, maybe that's all you should do. There ain't much to be cheerful about, is there?"

"No."

He didn't turn. "That's part of the trouble with you white guys. You're always trying to fill the silence. Sometimes I think you're afraid of it. So you talk too damn much." He paused, meditating. I started to say something, but stopped myself. He went on. "Ya, the big silence. I think maybe the old ones of our tribe understood it, but they're all gone now. . . . I don't have any sacred Indian wisdom for you, man, but I think a lot goes on that we can't understand. It's like, you know, there are things moving out there in the silence. They're talking to Sheila, inviting her to come with them. And she's listening. She's getting ready to go, and I don't think she wants a lot of talk right now." He turned to me, his dark eyes filled with pain. "She's resting up for the journey, man. All you can do is listen to the silence with her until she decides it's time to go." He turned back to the window.

197

I thought about it for a long minute. "Cripes, you should have been a medicine man."

He snorted. "Ya, I talk too damn much too." He sat and reached for the pack of cigarettes on the table. "Me not breaking training, Coach. Me making smoke with white friend. Old Indian custom." He lit a cigarette, took a puff, then studied the smoke from the cigarette. I lit another, and we sat in the silence until our cigarettes were finished. "Phil's down in the car," he said. "He wants to talk."

"About what?"

Mike shrugged. "Things. . . . He feels like hell about that falling-out you guys had."

"Why doesn't he come up here and say so?"

"He was going to, but then . . . I don't know; he just got real uncomfortable. Asked me to come up."

For a second, I felt like saying, "Well, screw him if he's not man enough to come himself." But instead, I reached for my coat. Mike lingered for a moment at the door to Sheila's room on our way out.

Near the car, Mike said, "I'm going to take a turn around the block. Check for buffalo sign."

I nodded, opened the passenger door, and slid in. "Hi, Phil."

"Hi. How's it going with Sheila?"

"It won't be very long now."

"I'm sorry. . . ." For a long minute he stared through the windshield at the hospital. "I should have come to see her," he said. "I just couldn't do it, Jerr. The thought of it just scared the hell out of me. . . . I'm sorry I was such a lousy friend. To her and to you."

I hunched my coat up around my shoulders. "I guess it wouldn't have changed much."

"Except we'd still be friends. . . . I guess that's what makes me feel the worst—that I was too yellow to save our friendship. But, Jerr, I just can't stand being around sick people. Even people with a cold or the flu or something. I don't want to catch anything."

"You don't catch what Sheila's got."

"Ya, but it could be me up there dying. I'm a coward about it. I just can't think about death."

"I'm sorry. I didn't know it upset you so much."

"Ya, well, it does. . . . But I still should have come to see her." He swung open the door hard. "Let's go."

I caught up with him halfway across the parking lot. "Phil, you don't have to do this. Even if she's awake, I don't think she even recognizes some people now." Phil kept going.

In the elevator, his face was pale, and he hesitated a long moment at Sheila's door before going in. He stood for two or three minutes by her bed with his hands folded in front of him like he was viewing the corpse at a funeral. Then he reached down and touched her hand. "Bye," he said softly.

Halfway down the hall, he turned in at the men's room. "I've got to take a whiz." The door closed, and I heard him vomit in a toilet. Poor Phil, I thought. Why hadn't he told me? Maybe he had.

At the elevator, I said, "Thanks, Phil. I'll tell Sheila you were here."

"Ya, sure. Hey, I've got to go. Mike's waiting." He stuck out a hand. "I'll see you around."

I sat by Sheila for a while longer, too tired to move. Maybe Bonnie would slip up for a moment after the banquet. I'd tell her what Mike had said. And about Phil. A nurse looked in and pointed to her watch—visiting hours were long over. I nodded, pried myself out of the chair, and gathered up my stuff.

When I kissed Sheila, she jerked, then relaxed. "Details," she murmured.

199

Bonnie came by a few minutes after I left. Sheila had seemed o.k. then, but her breathing changed in the night. One of Bonnie's nurse friends called her around seven in the morning. Bonnie called me. "Fran said Sheila's breathing is shallow, then deep, shallow, then deep."

"What does that mean?"

"Fran says it means that the end is getting close. There's probably brain damage already."

"I'll get right up there."

"Take it easy. I don't think you have to rush. Fran said this breathing pattern can last quite a while. I'll go in after breakfast. Why don't you bring Mrs. Porter around ten?" I agreed, hung up, and stood staring at the phone.

Melissa came into the kitchen. I shook myself and started getting some breakfast. "Is something happening?" she asked quietly.

I nodded. She didn't press me. We sat across from each other, eating cereal. After a couple of minutes, I told her what Bonnie had said.

Melissa kept her eyes on her cereal. "Then it's almost over. I'm glad; Sheila's suffered enough."

There was a big lump in my throat, and I could only nod.

When I left, Melissa gave me a hug. "Tell Mom when she gets home," I said. "Tell her I'm o.k. and not to worry."

Dr. Belke was with Bonnie and Sheila when Mrs. Porter and I arrived. He told us Sheila might go on like this for a few hours or a couple of days. Before he left, he stood staring down at her for a long minute, then laid his palm gently on her cheek.

The old lady sat by Sheila's bed for twenty minutes. We left them alone and talked in the lounge. Some new realities needed facing. When the old lady came out, we met her in the hall. "Mrs. Porter," Bonnie said, "have you thought about making any arrangements? Ah, you know, like calling a funeral director."

"Yes, dear." She patted Bonnie's arm. "I've got lots of experience. I've told the girls at the desk who to call. Don't worry." She started down the hall, then turned. Her eyes were clear, sharp—however briefly, she was fully back in the world. "Thank you for everything. My granddaughter was lucky to have such good friends." I started to follow, but she waved me back. "No, you stay, young man. I'll call a taxi."

We had lunch in the cafeteria, neither of us able to eat much, then sat through the early afternoon with Sheila. Bonnie fidgeted. Finally, she stood. "I've got to find something to do. Push the book cart around or something. I'll take over when you want to go for supper." I nodded.

After a while I turned on the TV and found a basketball game to watch. Beside me, Sheila's breathing continued shallow, then deep, then shallow again. Late in the afternoon, she started to miss a breath every once in a while. I called a nurse. "It's normal," she said.

Bonnie came back around five o'clock, looking tired, and I took a break. I drove downtown in the early dusk. The streets were wet with the runoff from thawing snowbanks. At the drive-in, I bought hamburgers, fries, and a Coke, then drove out along the river road north of town. I ate my supper sitting on a picnic table in the wayside park. The wind from the southwest blew warm. Long, wide streaks on the face of the river showed where the afternoon sun had melted the snow and softened the ice. Sheila will never see the river flow free again, I thought. Then I said aloud, "Shut up, Kinkaid. Don't think too much now. Just hang in there."

201

Bonnie was sitting with her back to the door, holding Sheila's hand. I stepped back into the hall and listened to Bonnie talking very softly. "I'm sorry, Sheila. I'm sorry you're dying, and I'm sorry I fell in love with him. But I couldn't help it. If you can hear any of this, don't be angry. You can't do anything more for him. But I can; I can love him, Sheila. I can love him just as well as you did. Please let him go, Sheila. Let him go, so he can love me too."

The Tiger put her head down on the covers and cried. I turned away and walked quietly down to the lounge. I smoked a cigarette and watched the night darken over the river. Bonnie came in. "Hi. You're back," she said.

"Ya, I stopped to burn one. How's she doing?"

"Her breathing's gotten rougher, I think. The nurse said her blood pressure is down a little, but that doesn't necessarily mean anything." She sat and lit a cigarette. "We smoke too much."

"Ya, I think I'm going to quit when this is over."

"Me too. . . . I don't suppose we could do that together? Mutual support and all that. We could plan that if we, ah, still have that deal to talk some things out."

"We've still got a deal."

She concentrated on thoroughly crushing the cigarette. "Mind if I go home for a while? I've got a brute of a headache."

"Go ahead. I'll call you if there's any change."

At the door, I put an arm around her. She hesitated, then put her arms around me. Her cheeks were wet. "Good night, Tiger," I said.

I watched the TV without really seeing what was on. Every time Sheila's breath skipped a few seconds, I'd wait, holding my own. Her breath kept coming back every time until about ten-thirty, when it stopped forever. I sat with her for a while longer, then tucked the covers up around her chin, and walked down to the nursing station to tell someone.

I did my crying on the way home. No sobs, just big, slow tears. I called Bonnie from the kitchen. "Sheila died just over an hour ago. Her breath just went and didn't come back."

There was a long pause. Bonnie let out a long, ragged sigh. "I'm sorry. . . . Do you want me to come over?"

"No. Not tonight. I'm just too tired to think. . . . Let's go for a walk tomorrow."

"I'd like that."

I hung up and sat for a long time in the darkened kitchen. Then I got up and walked onto the porch. I stood listening to the night. There was no crying on the wind, no words blown from beyond the silence. Just a night wind and the promise of spring.

FOURTEEN

The river split around an island, the right channel too rocky and shallow for the canoe, the left all spray and thunder as the river hurtled over a ledge. The current accelerated as I fought the glare of sun on water to find the downstream V of dark water marking the chute through the ledge. When I finally picked it out, we were too far to the right. "Left," I yelled. "We've got to get left." We dug hard. I drove the bow almost across the V, then leaned to my right as far as I dared, and jammed my paddle hard against the current. The stern kicked left and the bow swung perfectly into the point of the V. Then we were over, the bow plunging into the turbulence below the chute, then rearing like a bucking horse. In the bow, Bonnie whooped.

It was too early to celebrate. Ahead the river boiled around boulders, then over a smaller ledge. I swung the bow to the left, and we dug for all we were worth. I aimed at a big boulder, then swung back at the last second to hit the lower chute dead on. In a few more seconds, we were

205

gliding by the lower end of the island in quiet water. We were laughing uncontrollably.

We beached the canoe and climbed out. Bonnie threw her arms around me. "God, I love you."

"It sounds a little like a cliché, but I love you too, Tiger."

She spun. "Hear that, everybody! I'm loved by Jerry Kinkaid, the best guy in the whole world."

The memory of Sheila came back to me. For a moment, I stared over Bonnie's dark head at the river and the trees beyond. "What's the matter?" she asked quietly.

"Nothing. . . . Hey, I'm thirsty. Want a Coke?"

We spread a blanket and lay tanning in the sun. Bonnie stretched. "What a beautiful spot."

"I don't always take girls to scumbag motels."

She pounced on me. "Shut up! Don't always go reminding me of the stupid stuff I said!"

I laughed and held her. "O.k., o.k. I won't do it again, Tiger."

She lay with her head on my chest. After a long minute, she asked, "What were you thinking about after I yelled a while ago?"

"Sheila. She did something like that one time." I described that afternoon by the river so long ago.

"You did love her, didn't you?"

"In the end, I guess I did. . . . But I love you better."

"Good." She kissed me long and deep, then propped herself on her elbows and stared down into my eyes. "I think it's o.k. that we've ended up like this. I think she'd be happy for us."

"I know she would."

We lay in each other's arms. The Tiger flinched just before she fell asleep, and for a moment she held me a little tighter. Then she smiled and relaxed. I lay awake a little longer, breathing the warm smell of her, feeling the film of

206

sweat forming between our bodies. Tiger, Tiger, I thought.

A breeze came up when the sun began to edge below the treetops. We folded the blanket and tossed the empty cans into the bottom of the canoe. The Tiger climbed in the bow. I pushed the canoe out into the current and hopped in over the stern. The current took hold, swung us gently away from the shore, and together we let it take us downriver.